I0629996

BRIGGS

CASS

ALSO BY RON BRIGGS

Yellow Hair Series

Erik Haraldsson

Tor's Saga

CASS

YELLOW HAIR
BOOK THREE

RON BRIGGS

WOLFPACK
PUBLISHING
— EST 2013 —

Cass
Paperback Edition
Copyright © 2024 by Ron Briggs

Wolfpack Publishing
1707 E. Diana Street
Tampa, Florida 33609

www.wolfpackpublishing.com

All rights reserved. No part of this book may be reproduced in any form or by any electronic or mechanical means, including information storage and retrieval systems, without express written permission from the publisher, except for the use of brief quotations in reviews. Any use of this publication to train generative artificial intelligence (AI) technologies is expressly prohibited.

This book is a work of fiction. References to historical events, real people, or real places are used fictitiously. Any similarity to real persons, living or dead, is purely coincidental and not intended by the author.

All brand names and product names used in this book are trademarks, registered trademarks, or trade names of their respective holders. Wolfpack Publishing is not associated with any product or vendor in this book.

Paperback ISBN 979-8-89567-006-4
Ebook ISBN 979-8-89567-005-7
LCCN 2024947851

DEDICATION

This book is dedicated to the woman that inspired the character, Cass. She showed from a very young age that obstacles would not deter her from doing the things she found important. From completing a 22-mile bicycle ride for charity on a bicycle with training wheels—before reaching her fifth birthday; being the only child in her school to learn to play the oboe; despite her small stature, working hard to become a standout softball pitcher in high school and college; gaining success in kickboxing; completing several GoRuck events; earning a surgical RN position; the list goes on. Could not be prouder of my daughter!

CASS

CHAPTER 1
MASSACRE

Bright Moon peeked through spaces in the tumbled rocks wide-eyed and mouth agape. Frozen in fear, she could not believe what she was witnessing. In her eight summers, she had never been exposed to anything like the scene before her.

Her mother would deliver a new brother or sister in less than a moon, but there she was, forced onto her hands and knees while the brutal war chief from Black Bear Village rammed his huge manhood into her relentlessly. Bright Moon understood what rape was and that forcing a woman was punishable by banishment among the Monongahela People, her people. Yet his warriors were cheering him on, bringing him new victims while taking a few of their own.

1

As the afternoon wore on, Bright Moon was still able to see the blood on his penis as he pulled away from her mother after releasing his seed for the third time. Her mother, Head Matron Yellow Lotus, dropped to her side on the ground, holding her swollen belly and gritting her teeth in pain. Bright Moon knew her mother was too proud to give the evil warrior the pleasure of crying out.

Bright Moon had no way of knowing that the long night of torture, blood, and death was just beginning. She could only stare at the mayhem, listen to the screaming, crying, and moaning of the victims, quivering in fear as she pressed tightly against her aunt Water Mint's side. On the young woman's other side, Bright Moon's twin sister, Bright Star, pushed her trembling body into her aunt's protection.

Water Mint had only seen ten-and-six summers and was just as traumatized as her eight-summers-old nieces. Yellow Lotus was her sister, and watching helplessly while the rape and torture continued would scar her for life. Hidden as they were in the old, abandoned tunnel under the plaza, her biggest fear was that one of the children would cry out, exposing their location. She held both tightly to her sides, praying they felt protected by her.

Following his malicious act, Thunder Throat

stood over Yellow Lotus and demanded the location of Water Mint and the twin girls. When the hapless woman only stared at him defiantly, he violently kicked her in the breast. She shuddered but did not cry out. He walked over to where the twins' father, Black Wolf, husband of Yellow Lotus, was tied to the cross piece of the animal butchering rack next to the fire pit in the plaza of Long Pine Village.

"The Head Matron seems a little too distraught to answer my questions. If you value her life, and that worm excrement she harbors in that big belly, you better find your tongue!" Thunder Throat demanded, yelling in Black Wolf's ear. Bright Moon's father hung by his wrists with his feet tied to another log under him. His forehead was furrowed and beaded in sweat from bearing his pain in silence.

"Tell me where the woman is hiding the girls, and no one else needs to feel my wrath," the young enemy war chief said to Black Wolf.

"I, I can tell you nothing because, like my wife, we simply do not know. This is not about revenge. Your souls are loose," Black Wolf hissed. He was met with a fist to the gut that drove the wind from his lungs. Black Wolf nearly passed out before he could breathe again.

Bright Moon's eyes were filled with tears of

horror and sympathy for both her parents. Yet, she could not look away. If they could endure the pain, she could endure watching. Shaking, she pressed tighter against her aunt's taut body.

CHAPTER 2
A NEW NAME

*Y*ou will destroy *that man*, a deep, calm, man's voice sounded in Bright Moon's head.

W-what? Did I just hear a voice? Bright Moon was confused.

I am known by many names. You will know me as 'Wolf.' I am First Man. You have been chosen. I will guide you from time to time. You will grow strong and wise. When you are ready, I will tell you how you will complete the task I have given you, the voice answered.

I-I am just a girl, what can I do? I cannot be a warrior. Somehow, she knew the voice was hearing her thoughts.

You will become a warrior like your people have

never known. You are no longer 'Bright Moon.' From this night, until you finish your task, you will be known as 'Cass.' And your sister will be 'Pena.' You must avoid the Black Bear People and all the tricks Thunder Throat will employ to find you. Over several sun cycles you will get stronger and faster than any woman. When you have completed the task before you, power will decide what to do with you. Until then, you belong to me. Together we will destroy the evil that has invaded your world and bring harmony back to this valley, Wolf explained.

Water Mint felt Bright Moon's body relax. Thinking the girl had fallen asleep, she slowly bent over and peered into the child's face. The young girl's expression had changed from fear to determination, and her tears had dried. Bright Moon's gaze did not waver from Thunder Throat, as if studying him. Water Mint did not understand, but she knew there was a big change in the girl's demeanor. Bright Star continued to tremble, and tears streaked her cheeks.

Mother, Father, and our people should not suffer so. Why me? Why must my people wait for me to grow up before their suffering is avenged? Bright Moon, now Cass, sought to challenge the spirit who talked in her head.

Child, power has no interest in time or the

suffering of a few people. It is the balance between white and red, chaos and order. There is no timeline for such things. You must accept that you were chosen, and you must act accordingly. You can do nothing for these people tonight, but when you fulfill your destiny, these grievances will be made right, the voice responded without emotion.

Cass watched what she could through the tumbled rocks. The afternoon light faded, and darkness covered the ruined village. The black smoke from the burning lodges drifting across the plaza shifted to gray ghost-like swirls reflected by the firelight from the roaring central fire pit. The surviving Long Pine elders wore faces of total defeat. Most had hacked their hair in mourning for loved ones killed or captured.

Cass could hear Thunder Throat continue to question each Long Pine captive as to the whereabouts of Water Mint and the twin girls. The best she could tell was that no one had noticed the three of them returning to the Water Plant Clan Longhouse. She knew that few, if any, knew about the tunnel they were hiding in.

Cass looked to her mother's now lifeless body. She had been mercilessly raped and mutilated by Thunder Throat. He even sliced her swollen belly open and ripped out the unborn child. Then, before she died, he shoved a red-hot brand into her bleeding woman hole as a final insult. *Why had he hated her so?*

Her father fared no better. He lay with both shoulders dislocated, his mouth stuffed with his own genitals, his gut ripped open, and a long rope of his intestine burned in the fire pit. Mercifully, his suffering had ended when his life-soul fled his ruined body.

Long into the night, Cass could hear the whimpering and screaming of women or girls being raped. Gradually, the sounds lessened, and at last, she heard Thunder Throat's horrible voice order his men to be ready to move upriver at first light. The elders would be left to fend for themselves. The women and children captives would be guarded until they were loaded into canoes in the morning. The acrid smells of burning flesh, lodges, and possessions kept Cass from any restful sleep.

When morning light came, Cass was already awake and observing everything she could see. Smoke still sifted skyward from the smoldering lodges and other buildings that had made up Long Pine Village. Her parents' bodies had been unceremoniously tossed onto the roaring flames of the central fire pit.

The Black Bear warriors scurried around,

looking for valuables and preparing to depart. Finally, an angry and anxious Thunder Throat ordered a warrior named Black Cheek and fifteen others to protect their south flank on their return to Black Bear Village.

CHAPTER 3
SMALL REVENGE

B lack Cheek took the rear position, trusting himself more than any other warrior. He moved only when the others were out of sight, and then only from one tree to the next.

A hand of time after leaving the ruins of Long Pine Village behind, when the others were just out of sight, Black Cheek waited another finger of time before making his next move. He took a step when suddenly he felt a blow to the back of his right shoulder, and a bloody chert point protruded just below his collarbone. Before he stumbled to the ground, hard hands grabbed him up. A blurry warrior appeared in front of him. Black Cheek could only look on in disbelief. His mind and body were stunned, and his shoulder locked in place by the arrow through his shoulder blade.

He had never experienced this level of pain before. Not even when, while on his vision quest as part of his initiation into manhood, he fell on a sharp rock that ripped into his cheek. Before it began to heal, the whole left side of his face had turned black.

Now, he stood propped up by two warriors and was trying to understand what had happened to him. He could smell his own blood and the pain was unbearable, but he began to realize the wound was not fatal if he could get some help soon.

"Yarrow told you that you would regret killing my unborn child," Tallow calmly told Black Cheek, then added, "Of course I would have killed you for raping my wife anyway. I gave you that wound so you could linger long enough for Black Willow here to give you something more."

Tallow reached down and removed Black Cheek's war club and tossed it aside, then cut the cord that held the wounded warrior's breechclout to his waist. Tallow then took up Black Cheek's left arm, and the warrior previously holding it stepped in front of him.

Only then did Black Cheek realize the warrior was a woman. *How can it be?* he wondered. He had always been taught that women were forbidden from becoming warriors. Sure, there were stories and legends, but he had never known or seen one himself.

She stepped in front of him with a serious look on her face. "Why have the Black Bears gone on this war walk? What has happened in your village to change who you are so quickly?" she demanded.

He was stunned by the turn of events, and his mind was clouded by pain. Finally, he mustered the strength to answer her.

"Too long has there been peace in this valley. Our warriors were becoming weak from lack of war. The assassination of our war chief gave us a new leader. Great War Chief Thunder Throat, a real ruler, had a reason to make war on Long Pine Village. The ease with which we walked in and destroyed the Long Pines is testament to how weak the valley has become." He gritted his teeth against the pain after uttering the words Great War Chief Thunder Throat had ordered him to say if he was captured.

"But the Long Pine War Chief did not, would not, harm your war chief. He enjoyed and honored the peace in the valley. The treachery came from somewhere else. More than a moon past, an arrow went missing from our war chief's quiver. He thought he must have lost it, never suspecting treachery. I suspect that Thunder Throat, and maybe that weasel, Falcon, were behind the assassination of your war chief. Evil spirits dwell in their souls." Black Willow looked into his eyes, telling him that she saw the truth.

Black Cheek's strength was waning and now he saw in her eyes a promise to inflict more pain on him. His stomach churned in fear.

"Now, I have something for you, since you participated in the destruction of Long Pine Village and eagerly raped my younger sister, Yarrow. You need to feel the way she did when you brutally killed the life growing in her womb, then forced yourself upon her. On top of that, you were all too eager to take my son and others to become slaves in Black Bear Village. As a reward, I have this for you." She pulled her slender war club from her waist belt and ran her fingers along the shaft and over the carved wooden ball at the end.

She reached down and took his manhood in her hand, stretched it out, and quickly slammed the war club into the organ as she let go of it. The impact split the skin open, crushing the delicate fibers within. He let out a howl of pain. Next, she took a small, heart-shaped flat stone she had found and was saving in case this opportunity arose. She forced the stone into his quivering groin area so that his scrotum rested on the flat stone. Blood flowed from his shredded penis over his scrotum and the stone she used to support the testicles within. She then brought the war club violently down onto one of his testicles, crushing it completely. The prisoner was released, and he fell onto his knees and began vomiting violently. They left him there and headed back to the ruins of Long Pine Village. Black Willow cleaned her hand on tall vegetation as they made their way to the ruined village, looking for the surviving elders left by the Black Bear warriors. Coyotes or wolves would leave Black Cheek's ghost screaming in the darkness for eternity.

CHAPTER 4
REFUGEES

C ass, Pena, and Water Mint crawled toward the dim light filtering into the tunnel from the entrance that had been under Water Mint's bed platform. They could smell fresh air mixing in with the smoke and earthy odors in the tunnel. Most of the lodge and belongings had been burned away and the opening lay exposed. It was so small, no one had noticed it until the girls and young woman climbed out. They paused to sing a death song over the fire pit where the bodies of the Head Matron and War Chief had been rendered to white ash, then ran to the huddled elders, most of whom were weeping.

Cass caught movement, stiffened, then relaxed as she watched a string of Long Pine warriors, a few women, and children advancing cautiously toward them. Their leader appeared to be Hard Edge of the Wolf Clan and nephew of the murdered war chief.

With astonishment in his voice, Hard Edge asked Water Mint, "How can it be? How did you survive? And why did you come back?"

"We never left," she answered quietly. "We used the old tunnel to hide in and witnessed the whole thing. It was hard, but the girls did remarkably well, considering."

"What did you say? What tunnel?" Hard Edge demanded.

"There was an old tunnel under the Head Matron's lodge that led to the pile of rocks in the plaza. I was told it had once been used in ceremonies. I thought everyone knew of it," she answered calmly. He just shook his head in disbelief.

"Bright Moon, Bright Star, I am sorry you had to endure last night. We were vastly outnumbered and could only watch from the shadows," Hard Edge said as he took their small hands in his.

"From this day forward, I am known as *Cass*, Bright Moon is no longer," Cass replied in a cold, distant voice, then added, "It was endured as it was meant to be. A spirit spoke to me and told me, one day, I will kill Thunder Throat. My sister, who is now known as *Pena,* will assist me in this task."

Tallow gave Water Mint a questioning look. She just shrugged and gave him a look that said, *Do not be surprised.*

In all, Hard Edge and Tallow brought twelve warriors, four young men who had never seen battle before, six women, and four children who had seen less than ten summers. Together they gathered the elders and the very few items they were able to salvage from the smoking, ruined lodges and went to the canoe landing. They were able to patch and repair enough canoes to transport the whole party by water to Monongahela Village where they hoped they would be welcomed as refugees.

CHAPTER 5
MONONGAHELA VILLAGE

Five days later, Water Mint, Cass, and Pena stood before Head Matron Corn Stalk and the Council of Elders in Monongahela Village. Corn Stalk said, "You two are the heirs of Long Pine Village. We will help you determine what you intend to do about that. And your names are Bright Moon and Bright Star. Changing your names would be a dishonor to your mother, my beloved niece. I will not have you take slave names in her absence." Corn Stalk looked to Water Mint for support.

Cass replied, "May we talk to you strictly in private, Head Matron? For our mother's sake?"

"That would be highly unusual, but I suppose I can accommodate the request under the circumstances," Corn Stalk was taken aback by the level of maturity and composure these eight-summers-old children were showing. She led the girls and their aunt from the Council of Elders meeting into her private chamber in the Corn Clan longhouse.

When they were completely alone, Corn Stalk said, "Bright Moon, I believe you seem to be the spokesperson for you and your sister. Please tell me why this meeting needs to be private."

"Head Matron, six nights past, my sister and I witnessed a great many evil and horrendous things. It changed us forever. While hiding in that tunnel, I was visited by more than a spirit helper. Wolf—First Man, himself, told me that I will kill Thunder Throat and that my sister will help make that happen. He said that I must dedicate my life to getting faster, stronger, quicker, and smarter in battle than any human who ever lived. I know our traditions frown on women warriors, but my sister and I have been chosen for that role.

"And I know that Thunder Throat is offering a reward for anyone who turns any of us, including Water Mint, over to him. We cannot let that happen. I ask that we assume roles as household slaves here while we learn to become great fighters. One day, somewhere, I will meet Thunder Throat on a battlefield, and I will kill him. It is my destiny. But if we continue in our old identities, he will find us, and he will treat us as slaves before he kills us. He promised that. I vowed, in that tunnel, that we would see our mother, father, and the rest of Long Pine Village avenged. I, we, ask that you not stand in the way of us fulfilling our destiny."

Corn Stalk huffed, then answered, "You are but a child. How can you understand what you ask? I have never heard of anyone who wanted to grow up to be a murder weapon. You are just full of emotion. In time you will settle with your role as a clan maid and later a matron. You must learn that your first duty is to your clan. You can have any number of warriors fulfill your promise to kill Thunder Throat.

"We will help you rebuild Long Pine Village with the survivors, and by the time you become a woman, you can assume your destiny as a matron of the Water Plant Clan. In the meantime, we will protect you here so that you can grow up safe and sound. Now let us arrange for some new clothes and space here. Of course, all three of you are welcome in this lodge. Water Mint, you seem quiet and distant. You must help me make these girls understand." She could see that the young girls were not to be persuaded by her words.

"I was in that tunnel with these two. I saw and heard what they did. It changed us all. And I am very aware of the traditions of our people, but I also understand the girls' reaction. I feel powerless to do it myself, but I believe Cass when she says Wolf visited her. Her whole expression changed from abject fear to one of solid resolve. Her tears dried up, and her demeanor went from young girl to young warrior. I promised to help her make this happen. It would not be hard for you to send us all to some place down the Spirit River for our protection. Then acquire new slaves, say from the Tenasee peoples, to work in your house. Do you see how this could work?" Water Mint answered.

"Now you are sounding strange! Do you think I could send these two, no matter how much they trained as warriors, out to fight a man like Thunder Throat? It would be a death sentence. We must put an end to this silly notion." Corn Stalk was adamant.

"Head Matron," Cass began, "no one is asking you to be responsible. Our world was destroyed by some evil spirit force." She spread her arms to include her sister and her aunt. She spoke far beyond her eight summers. "We cannot have normal lives, merely grow up, be maidens and matrons. We were spared for a special reason. Given the spirit that came to me, I believe, together, we can make our world again—by destroying the evil that invaded that night. I have no idea how long it may take, but I think it is up to us to make the world right again. According to

Wolf, I was chosen by power. That cannot be ignored or denied. We must be given the chance." Water Mint and Pena looked at her and nodded approval as they held hands in unity.

"For the life of me, I do not understand, but I can see how important this is to all of you. Let me ponder it, and we will settle on a plan later. In the meantime, do not leave this lodge. The fewer people who see you now, the better to make something work." Corn Stalk, for one of the few times in her life, felt helpless.

CHAPTER 6

HERMITS

"**W**here is Black Cheek?" Thunder Throat demanded.

"He never caught up to us after we left Long Pine Village and dispersed along the south trail, Great War Chief," replied Big Cat. Big Cat is the grandson of the late War Chief Panther, who had first welcomed Strong Bear, Thunder Throat's father, to Black Bear Village. Big Cat was a strong and resourceful warrior. "We thought he had his reasons for lagging. He said not to look for him, that he would come when he was sure no Long Pine warriors followed us. I expected him by now, though."

"Take a party of ten and see if you can find him. If he is captured, he might say too much. Make sure he does not," Thunder Throat ordered.

———

TEN-AND-FIVE DAYS LATER, Big Cat reported to Thunder Throat, "Near sunset four days after we set out, we found what was left of a human carcass in a sparsely wooded glen southeast of the Long Pine Village ruins. Coyotes had ripped it apart and eaten most of the meat and all the soft parts. The skull was several paces away from the torso. We were not certain it was even the missing warrior. A broken arrow shaft was found, piercing a human shoulder blade. Our party searched for two hands of time but found no human tracks or signs. The coyotes had obviously dragged the body from the original kill site, dismembering it as they fought over it.

"Just before we gave up and headed to search the Long Pine Village site, a young warrior called out from the base of a large chestnut tree many tens of paces from the shoulder blade we found. The missing warrior's war club was lying close to the tree. No rain had fallen since the massacre, and much of the evidence was still present. Old blood spots were abundant on the ground and dried on the tree trunk. A warrior, most likely the one we searched for, had been wounded. He had been down on one good hand and knees vomiting, laid down, then got to his feet, and tried to move. He had gotten only a few paces when, judging by the blood smeared on the tree, he tried to climb. That was where the coyotes attacked him.

"Other people had been around the tree where our missing friend had been wounded. At least one set of tracks belonged to a woman. Many coyote tracks were on top of the human tracks, making our search difficult. At last, we found a group, including some children, had set out from near that tree in the general direction of Long Pine Village, but the tracks soon disappeared. These people knew how to travel without being followed. Our party put all the bones we could find in one of the warriors' bags and set out for Long Pine Village. We could surely overpower a few warriors, women, and the remaining elders.

"By the time we got to Long Pine Village the following day, it was deserted. We made a cold camp outside the village ruins so we would not disturb any restless ghosts and posted guards over night. In the morning, while searching the ruins, we discovered the opened entrance to an old tunnel and determined that a woman and two children had been in there, possibly during the great victory over the Long Pines. The big fire pit no longer smoked and had been picked through by someone. There appeared to be no bones to gather. Several fresh graves had been dug around the burned longhouses. Down by the river, six or seven canoes had been repaired and slid into the water, headed downstream. Among those climbing into the canoes were a few light-footed women and six children."

Thunder Throat was furious as Big Cat finished his report.

———

WARRIORS DISGUISED as traders and other spies dispatched by Thunder Throat found no fugitives in Monongahela Village or anywhere that came close to fitting the descriptions of Water Mint, Bright Moon, and Bright Star. Among the many rumors that were on every tongue was that three fugitives fled from Monongahela Village fearing they would be betrayed. They left in secret, and no one knew for sure if they went up the Mononga- hela River or down the Spirit River. Monongahela Village was located where the Monongahela and Spirit Water Rivers converge to form the Spirit River. Three canoes were said to be missing, and no other credible information was given. Some suggested they may have gone back to the ruins of Long Pine Village.

———

IF ONE CANOED a hand of time upstream on the Monongahela River from Monongahela Village, left the river, and followed an obscure game trail south adjacent to a small creek to the eroded valley wall, they would find, behind a screening wall of rock that had separated from the cliff, a tangle of fallen trees and brush. A closer look would find a snug lodge under the pile of logs. In that lodge lived a young hermit fisherman with twin *boys* about eight-summers old. They belonged to no clan and were seldom seen except by a certain warrior who had been a fugitive from Long Pine Village.

Most days he would meet the hermit and the two *boys*. The small party would go to various secret locations where the *boys* would train tirelessly in the skills of warriors. They would also race each other and the warrior. The training included tracking and stealth techniques. They were determined to become the most lethal warriors who ever lived. They would need to be.

CHAPTER 7
TRAINING BEGINS

Tallow was troubled. It had been a moon since his life was torn apart and left in shattered ruins. He and Yarrow had been expecting their first child before the Moon of Deep Snow. Now, she was gone; raped and stolen away by Black Bear warriors. A hard punch to her abdomen had ended her pregnancy in a brutal fashion just before they had raped her the first time.

He could not see what happened to her. He was hiding with the other warriors and some escapees out beyond the village in thick vegetation. They were vastly outnumbered and watched in stunned silence as Thunder Throat carried out his unthinkable massacre of Long Pine Village.

Now, Tallow found himself sitting on a log

next to the beautiful Water Mint as they watched the twins, Cass and Pena, race around a large meadow, working to make their young bodies stronger. *How did I get here? Why me?* he asked the Creator.

Water Mint wore a plain, sleeveless doeskin dress that came down below her knees and tied around her slim waist with a brown fabric sash knotted above her left hip. On the warm, sunny day, the girls wore only doeskin loin cloths and soft moccasins. All three had their hair chopped in varying lengths in mourning for their loved ones.

Tallow felt guilty that he had been spared while his young wife had not. She was being held against her will by vicious warriors who, little more than a moon past, he considered friends. She was being subjected to unspeakable horrors while he was sitting next to one of the most pleasant young women in the world.

Water Mint was beautiful, no doubt, and Tallow felt as if he was being unfaithful to Yarrow by even noticing. The young woman's eyes betrayed her own horrors. She had been a close-up witness to the destruction of Long Pine Village.

Tallow cleared his head and stood as the girls approached the finish line. He wore a simple buckskin vest, a Wolf Clan breechclout, and plain ankle-high moccasins. His hair had also been chopped in a random pattern with his own knife. The wolf paw print tattoos on his temples and forehead stood out more with his hair oddly chopped. He did not care.

As usual, the girls were stride-for-stride, neither one willing to finish second. He was impressed with the determination the girls were showing. Acting on instructions from Corn Stalk, Head Matron of Monongahela Village, and all the Monongahela People, he was working the girls extraordinarily hard. Corn Stalk believed the work would be too hard, and they would give up the silly notion of becoming warriors.

Instead, they were relishing the long hours, exceeding all expectations. It seemed they were becoming stronger and faster each time Tallow worked with them. A few days past, he had laid out ten large flat rocks on a line for each of them. Twenty paces away was another line. He had told them when he came back, he wanted each of them to have moved their rocks to the other line. He knew each rock weighed about as much as each of them, and they would not be able to move those rocks until they grew much older. To his astonishment, when they arrived at the meadow that day, all the rocks were in their new places.

"How could you move those rocks so fast? You must have gotten some help somehow. Water

Mint, did you help these girls move those rocks?"
Tallow asked.

"I did not!" Water Mint replied.

"It was her idea," Pena said and pointed to
Cass.

He looked at Cass with a questioning look on
his face.

"First, I tried to push one of the rocks. It would
not even wiggle. Then, I bent over and tried to lift
it. I could barely tip it. Pena laughed and said, 'Too
bad your arms are not as strong as your legs!' That
was when I got the idea to squat down, grasp the
rock with straight arms, and lift straight up with
my legs. I got it up, between my thighs and
hobbled over to the other line and dropped it. I lost
my balance and fell, but I got it there. After that,
Pena moved her first one the same way. Eventually
we were able to hold the rocks a little to the front,
and the others went faster and easier," Cass
explained.

Tallow was stunned. "Care to demonstrate?"
he asked, still not believing the young girls could
move the heavy rocks.

"Sure." Cass walked over to her woven grass
bag and pulled out a strip of rawhide about a
hand's width wide. She pushed the strip around
the sides of the rock to protect her fingers from its
rough texture. Next, she squatted down, lifted the

heavy rock, held it precariously in front of her, elbows barely bent, waddled over to the other line, bent her legs again, and set the rock down right where it had been three days prior.

Tallow just shook his head. "Corn Stalk will never believe it," he mumbled to no one. He noted Water Mint's proud smile. *By the Creator, she has a beautiful smile!* He kept the thought to himself.

"All right, girls, are you ready for some races?" Tallow asked, expecting protests.

"Are you going to race us?" Cass asked with a coy smile.

Tallow looked at Water Mint, who smiled and shrugged. He had marks at five-tens of paces, ten-tens of paces, and two-tens-of-tens of paces. First, they ran the longest sprint, then, the middle, finally, the shortest. He found he had to give it all he had to stay ahead in the first two races. The third had him and Pena crossing the line at the same time with Cass a half a step ahead. Again, Tallow was stunned.

After the workout, the sun was getting close to the western horizon. By the time they got to the hidden shelter, there was little light in the forest. Tallow looked at Water Mint sheepishly.

"We will make room for you, Tallow. No need in trying to navigate the river in the dark. Just keep your clothes on, turn your back to me, and keep your hands to yourself!" Water Mint told Tallow. Then she thought about Yarrow and turned red. In the darkness, no one saw her red face or Tallow's tear-filled eyes.

"We're going up to the pool to wash the dust and sweat off us," Cass announced as she and Pena slid through the door opening into the darkness.

Water Mint looked at Tallow and said, "I am so sorry. That was very insensitive of me. You must think I am a terrible person."

"No offense taken. You are nervous, and we are all in pain. Think nothing of it," Tallow replied, but she could hear the pain in his voice.

"We have all lost so much," she sighed, as tears began to slide down her cheeks.

Tallow wrapped his arms around her and silently held her against his warm body. She smelled his sweaty musk and melted against his muscular chest. She felt safe for the first time since the raid. They held each other tight until they heard the girls coming back.

They quickly pulled apart, and she nervously said, "I just have some jerky to offer. It is too warm for a fire in here."

"T-that would be fine," he stammered.

Cass acted as if she didn't notice a thing, but Pena could feel the tension between Water Mint and Tallow, though she could not understand it.

Before long, the night cooled, and everyone settled into their sleeping skins. The night was not half over when Cass bolted straight up. She was sweating and tears flowed down her cheeks. Pena hugged her and said, "It's all right, I am right here." Cass settled down, and everyone went back to sleep. A hand of time later, Pena came up out of her blankets in a similar manner.

"Typical night," Water Mint whispered to Tallow.

The next morning, Tallow announced he had duties in the village and would not be back for six or seven days. Each of the females blamed themselves for Tallow's extended absence.

CHAPTER 8

ALMOST CAUGHT

J ust because Tallow was gone for several days, Cass and Pena did not slow down for a moment. They continued their endurance, speed, and strength training using the techniques Tallow had taught them. They moved the rocks back and forth and found that task getting easier.

Then a weather change brought violent thunderstorms, heavy rain, and colder air with blustery northwest winds for three days. Being confined during that time, Cass busied herself building a bow to replace the one her father had made her that was lost in the raid.

Pena noticed Water Mint's quietness and somber mood. While Cass worked away trying to take all the irregularities from her bow with a piece of sandstone, Pena stood by Water Mint who pretended she was watching.

"Are you well, Aunt?" Pena asked.

When Water Mint did not respond, Pena put her arm around the young woman and pulled her tight to herself.

"What is it?" Water Mint asked like she was surprised.

"That is what I am asking you. You have been distant all morning." Thunder continued to rumble in the background, and rain drummed all around their small lodge.

"It is just this miserable weather—so depressing," Water Mint answered, not looking Pena in the eye.

"I think there is more than that. Are you thinking about—?" It was not necessary to finish.

"What? No. I was, um, no, it...it is nothing," Water Mint stammered.

"Tallow will be back soon enough," Cass said quietly as she felt a slight irregularity on the upper limb of her bow, rubbed the sandstone over it, then blew the dust away from the spot.

Pena looked at Cass and shook her head. *Who knew she heard a word we were saying.*

"There is nothing between Tallow and me! He is still married until we know what the Black Bears have done to Yarrow. We are all grieving and just trying to get to the next day. Tallow is just here to help you. He has no interest in me. And I would never ask him to betray my good friend, Yarrow," Water Mint insisted. *Poor Tallow, he is so lost. I do not have feelings for him, do I?*

"Of course," Cass said, finding another minute flaw on her new bow and fixing it without looking up.

After the rain stopped, the trails, meadows, and forest were much too wet to move around, but Cass was too tired of being confined to their small lodge. She convinced Pena and Water Mint to go down to the river and take the canoe out to do some exploring along the watercourse. They donned their tattered "hermit" clothes and headed out.

Rather than turning up the Monongahela toward River Birch Village, which was very close, they went up the Youghiogheny River. It was a longer distance upriver to Red Elk Village, which was smaller, providing fewer chances of running into anyone.

They had paddled upstream for about two hands of time and decided they would turn around after the next bend to return to their lodge. They were talking about what a lovely day it was for a canoe trip on the river. The recent rains had turned the rivers muddy, but in this stretch the flow was unaffected by the increased runoff from the storms.

Suddenly, a canoe loaded with four warriors came around the bend they were angling toward. As soon as the warriors saw them, they started paddling hard to get to the hermit's craft. All three girls wanted to panic and flee, but they had nowhere to go. They could not possibly outrun four big men, either back down the river or through the wet forest.

"Just act casual and let me do the talking. Remember, you are boys named Acorn and Pecan, and I am Chinquapin. We live off in the woods, alone," Water Mint warned. She was glad she had made them smear mud on their faces and wear their floppy hats that cast dark shadows on their faces.

When the warriors got close, they could see they were Black Bear Village warriors, no doubt looking for them.

"Greetings, strangers," Water Mint called to the other boat, in her friendliest *man* voice.

The canoe pulled alongside and stuck a paddle out to snag the two boats together.

"Who might you be on this river this fine day?" the apparent leader asked, looking curiously at Water Mint, then looking close at both Cass and Pena.

"My name is Chinquapin. My brothers and I live on the river and were looking for some promising catfish holes on this stretch. We live alone and are not part of any clan." She hoped her lowered voice sounded convincing.

"Young to be living alone on a river, are you not?" the big man asked.

"We get by."

"You must have come from a village at some time."

"Long as I can remember, we just lived on the river."

"Where are your mother and father?"

"Mother died six or seven sun cycles past, trying to have a baby. Both died. Our father died when he fell through the ice on the river last winter."

"All right. We are looking for a young woman and two young girls. They would be about your sizes. Have you seen anyone like that?"

"I have not. We do not see many people to talk to. Canoes travel up and down the river all the time. Where they from?"

"Up the Spirit Water some distance."

"You are the first person I have talked to since before our father died. How long have they been missing?"

"He does not know anything. Let's move on," said one of the other warriors.

Without another word, the leader unhooked his paddle, and they proceeded downriver.

Water Mint started paddling upstream again. "We better not turn downriver for a while."

"Going to be dark soon," Pena said, a worried look on her face.

"After dark it will be easier to avoid being seen," Cass replied.

"Where did you get that idea?" Water Mint asked.

"It just makes sense," Cass answered.

"Do you think we can find our creek in the dark?" Pena asked.

"I can," said Cass confidently. She figured the big rock on the bank just east of their creek would be visible, even in the faint starlight.

They waited a hand of time after full darkness covered the river, then started back downstream. They saw no other canoes on the Youghiogheny and went straight to the far bank of the Mononga- hela. They moved downriver, trying to be as silent as possible. They had less than a hand of time left before reaching their little creek when they spotted a campfire in the brush on the north side of the river. They passed by as quietly as possible.

Suddenly a voice yelled out from the bank near

the camp, "Black Knife! It's those fishermen! Looks like they are sneaking down the south bank!"

"Everyone up! After them! I knew that talker was lying!"

Water Mint knew there was a big sweeping bend to their right just ahead, then their creek was just past the point on the other side of that bend, on the left bank. The girls and Water Mint put their backs into paddling as hard as they could. They were just rounding the bend when they heard the warriors shove off and start after them. It would be close.

They reached their creek, and Cass identified it correctly. They got the canoe in and hid just when they heard the cursing warriors clearing the bend. They could not risk running on the muddy bank for fear of leaving tracks, and they would splash too loudly going up the mud-bottomed creek, so they hunkered in the thick brush where their canoe was hidden.

The warriors were frantically paddling for the next sweeping bend in the river, thinking the fugitives were going to Monongahela Village. They went by the small creek without a glance as they tried to head them off before reaching the big canoe landing.

———

THE BLACK BEAR warriors checked every canoe at the landing, paying attention to each one that was wet. They saw three people getting out of a canoe and thought they had their quarry. When one tall and two burly hunters stood up and lifted an elk carcass from their canoe, the warriors were convinced it was not the young woman and the twin girls they sought.

The four warriors ran up the packed-mud trail and through the palisade opening to enter Monongahela Village. They looked around, and seeing no one, proceeded to the plaza, which glowed in the light of the central fire pit.

Tallow was standing there talking to War Chief Wolf Master. Tallow was telling the war chief of the rapid progress of his apprentice *warriors*. Wolf Master seemed unimpressed.

"My son, Oak, would put them to shame," the war chief said.

Just then the Black Bear warriors walked up. Without so much as a greeting, Black Knife demanded, "A woman and two young girls just came into this village. Where are they?" He was catching his breath as he talked.

Wolf Master looked the man up and down, then scrutinized his companions. "First, you better learn some manners before you come into this village and start making demands of the war chief!

Second, you have no permission to ask to see any women in this village. And, last, if I still must look upon your ugly face in a finger of time, you will draw your last breath. Now, turn around and leave Monongahela Village and do not show your face until your Head Matron sends a peace party here to mend the harm your people caused!"

Wolf Master waved a subtle hand signal and eight armed warriors suddenly appeared. "Red Crow, escort these Black Bear maggots to their canoe and send them upriver. I do not care how dark it is. And do not listen to any of their complaints," the Chief ordered his squad leader.

"Thunder Throat will not tolerate this kind of treatment of his warriors," Black Knife warned Red Crow as they paddled away from the canoe landing in the dark. Only a sliver of the moon had appeared in the southeastern sky.

CHAPTER 9

NIGHTMARES

Cass walked as quietly as she could along the deer trail just a short distance from their lodge. She peeked around the next turn, and there was a cottontail just ahead facing away from her, munching on something green it handled in its front paws. She slowly pulled her new bow up, an arrow nocked and held to the sinew bowstring with her right hand. Just before she had the bow up and started to aim, the rabbit bolted off the trail. *What did I do wrong?* she asked herself.

She was walking, slump-shouldered, just outside the entrance of their small lodge when she heard Tallow coming up the trail from the river. After not seeing him for seven days, she was suddenly ecstatic, and missing a chance at a kill with her new bow was momentarily forgotten.

Tallow walked up to her, pointed to her weapon, and said, "What is this? I did not think you were ready to handle weapons yet. Who made the bow for you?"

"I made it, but I am not ready for it yet," Cass confessed, then told him about the rabbit as she looked at the ground.

"Let us talk about that later. Are the others in the lodge?"

"Yes, waiting another day for you to show up!"

"I am glad I was delayed, as it turns out."

Once in the lodge, there were mixed greetings all around. Cass and Pena were anxious to get back to supervised training and were upset that Tallow was a day later than he said he would be. Water Mint was so happy he came back, she had tears in her eyes. She wanted to hug the man but knew she must restrain herself.

"Something occurred in the village last night that you all need to be aware of," Tallow started, a serious expression on his face. "Four Black Bear warriors came up to the central fire pit. I happened to be there talking to War Chief Wolf Master. The Black Bear leader came right up and demanded that a woman and two young girls who had just entered the village were to be turned over to them. He offered no greeting and no explanation about his demand. Wolf Master had him escorted from the village and sent on their way. I do not know where they went, or if they are still looking. Can any of you tell me why this may have occurred?" His inquiring eyes met all three of them.

"My fault," Cass offered. "It was so nice yesterday, and we have been stuck in this small lodge for days. I knew the trails were still muddy, and we would leave tracks, so I suggested we go in the canoe along the river. Those men saw us, but Water Mint convinced them we were not who they searched for. It got dark, and we were coming back. They had a camp and saw us on the river and came after us. We got hidden in the creek just before they came by. We never saw them again."

"We all need to reflect on the seriousness of this. Those Black Bear warriors looked dangerous. And just because they left that canoe landing does not mean they just went back to Black Bear Village. They think they saw you, and they will hunt for you until they are satisfied that they did not. Do you understand? They could be checking every hand length along the river and scouring the forest for your tracks. You cannot afford to be found, and they will not give up. I think you should consider coming into the village for protection for a time, until they give up their search."

"Tallow, that sounds like Corn Stalk's words. How about we learn to use weapons we can defend ourselves with instead?" Cass replied.

"Cass, you are a child. You cannot yet wield any weapon that will protect you from Thunder Throat's determined warriors. No, you must concede, at least for a couple sun cycles, that you cannot defend yourself. You need to come in for your protection," Tallow ordered.

"Water Mint and Pena can move into the village. I will not. I will stay out of sight and not be found, but I will not come into the village," Cass replied with finality.

Tallow looked to Water Mint for support. He saw none. He only saw a distance between them. Before there was a longing. He had sensed that she was interested in him. That was gone now. He felt helpless.

"Wolf Master thinks that me coming out here on a regular basis will draw unwanted attention. The creek we use for a canoe landing will look 'used' and will alert the Black Bear warriors to begin snooping around here. He is right. Can you not understand that?" Tallow pleaded with the trio.

"Then we will not use the creek for a canoe landing. You can follow a game trail from the village, and we will stay off the river for a time." Cass would not concede moving into the village.

Tallow threw up his arms in defeat. "I thought this was how this conversation would go. Make sure you always wear your dirty hermit clothes with those floppy hats. Do not go anywhere unless you must and stay away from the river for now. I plan to stay here for several days to keep an eye on things." He watched a smile form on Water Mint's scowling face. That gave him a warmth deep in his stomach he did not expect.

Cass and Pena observed Tallow and Water Mint's faces and smiled at each other.

"Just do not forget what I have said here today," Tallow emphasized. Then he opened his pack and brought out a large deer rump for roasting. "We should eat well for a day or two, anyway." He grinned as he presented the big chunk of meat to Water Mint. She immediately went to work preparing to get it cooking.

"Now, let me see this bow you made, and you can tell me why you are not ready to use it yet," Tallow addressed Cass.

Cass handed him the bow. Pena was torn between helping Water Mint with the roast or listening to Tallow and Cass talk about her bow. She decided to help Water Mint.

Tallow examined the bow. "You used a

chokecherry stem and made your arrows from the same wood. Good choice for now. When you get older and stronger, you will need stronger wood such as elm for your bow. You have done a fine job shaping and smoothing the limbs. It looks like it will send an arrow plenty fast enough to kill a rabbit or a woodchuck. Of course, it will handle squirrels just fine. A raccoon, bobcat, fox, or coyote are tougher. Let me see your arrows."

Cass told him, again, about the rabbit that she had frightened away in the morning, missing her chance. She handed him her quiver.

"You just need to learn more about the animals. Rabbits' eyes are located where they can see all the way around themselves. You need to move only when something is between you and them, or when they are looking at something else. You will not get a shot at every one you see, but when you know what they can see or smell, you can put yourself in a better position to be successful with anything you hunt."

She smiled in understanding.

"You found good, straight stems for your arrows, did a fine job sanding them to a sharp point, even heat-treated the points so they would be harder and hold their sharpness longer. But you did not heat treat the whole shaft and use a straightener. See how some are starting to bend?

The wood takes water from the air and that causes the arrow shaft to warp and bend. That can be fixed by heating each arrow through and through, then working the bends straight with a tool. A moose antler with holes drilled through it works very well. I will show you how to make one."

Tallow went to a bluff where he could see the river, at least between the bends where their small lodge was located and stayed there all afternoon. He did not return until after dark. He saw no canoes that looked like they were occupied by the Black Bear warriors.

When he returned, the lodge was filled with the mouthwatering aroma of the roasting venison. Water Mint dished out carved bowls of the deer meat with boiled arrowhead and cattail root. A low fire provided soft yellow light and kept them warm as the outside temperature dropped when the sun went down. It never got cold, but it was much cooler than the day had been.

When it came time to sleep, Cass and Pena crawled under their sleeping robes and were soon sound asleep. Water Mint and Tallow looked at each other with fear, worry, and expectation in their eyes.

"It feels wrong to invite you to my bed, but it feels wrong not to," Water Mint confessed to Tallow.

"I feel the same way. I feel it is wrong, like I would be betraying Yarrow, even if they have already killed her. At the same time, I feel drawn to you in a way I cannot even explain," he answered honestly.

"Perhaps, at least for now, we could share our blankets but not our bodies?" she suggested.

"That would be better than sleeping out on the ground, but that is what I will do if you wish."

"No, it will be hard, but we can sleep back-to-back. I promise I will not tempt you—if you promise not to tempt me."

"That is probably the best we can do. Perhaps it will be different in the future."

"Agreed."

Water Mint crawled under her elk skin sleeping blanket and turned her back to Tallow, who crawled under the same hide with his back to her. Sometime around midnight, a nightmare invaded her sleep. Tallow wrapped her in his arms to comfort her. She cried until she fell back to sleep.

A bit later, Pena let out a blood-curdling scream and sat straight up. Cass was up in an instant, caressing Pena's sweaty forehead and using soothing words to calm her down. Soon both girls drifted back to sleep.

Water Mint told Tallow she was sorry and

turned away from him. He tried to ease her sobbing, but she pushed him away.

Shortly, Pena felt Cass shaking and jerking in her sleep. It was her turn to hold Cass and ease her back to sleep.

Water Mint awoke when a dim shaft of light appeared in the smoke hole. She was shocked to find herself plastered against Tallow's broad back. She fit into every curve of his body, and his warmth made her want to stay. But she felt it was wrong and pulled away. He awoke and climbed out of the sleeping pallet, standing up so fast it made him dizzy. They looked at each other in the dim light, smiled, and shrugged.

Water Mint climbed out of the sleeping pallet and went to work coaxing the fire back to life so she could get some tea started.

Cass went out the door hanging quickly without saying a word. Pena looked around, remembering she had woken everyone up in the middle of the night, and apologized for disturbing everyone's sleep.

"None of us get through a night without nightmares, Pena. It is just something we do," Water Mint replied, trying to sound in control. She turned to Tallow about the time Cass came back in after her personal ablutions were taken care of. Pena rushed out when Cass came in. Cass followed

Pena back out, bow and quiver in hand, giving Water Mint and Tallow a moment.

"I cannot ask you to stay in this lodge. We go through these nightmares every night. It is not fair to ask you to put up with it," Water Mint said weakly, a tear trickling down her cheek.

"How about letting me be the judge of that. There was plenty of horror to go around that night. Dreams invade my sleep sometimes, too. Just the thought of what we did to that lagging warrior turns my stomach. Not to mention what I envision has happened to my wife. Perhaps you and I can be of some comfort to each other. We do not need to add the pressure of coupling any time soon."

She stepped to him and wrapped her arms around him, and he held her like he would never let her go.

Pena came in, saw them hugging, said she was sorry, turned, and went back out into the cool morning air.

Water Mint finally stepped away from Tallow, added some ground rose hips, mint, and ground dried blackberries to the hot water, and let it simmer while she heated up part of the leftover venison.

They were just filling their bowls when Cass came flying through the door hanging, holding up the first rabbit she had taken with her new bow.

Her smile stretched from ear to ear, cheering everyone's morning.

AFTER SPENDING four days in their miserable, small camp enduring thunderstorms and heavy rain, Black Knife and his party spent the next several days patrolling up and down the Monongahela and Youghiogheny rivers looking for the canoe that they had detained. They were convinced it was the young woman and the twins from Long Pine Village who had eluded capture.

The Black Bear warriors spent hands of time paddling up and down the water courses and searching every creek that entered the Mononga-hela between the confluence with the Youghiogheny and Monongahela Village but found no tracks and no signs that a canoe had been in those channels. The warriors walked some of the trails along the riverbanks, and they found no suspicious signs there either. They maintained their camp above the confluence for several days and nights, finding no more clues, compounding their frustration and increasing the fear of being caught by Monongahela Village warriors.

"Do you think Thunder Throat will give us

credit for our effort?" a young warrior named Sharpshinned asked.

"Why would he do that? We have failed. We should have pressed them harder when we had them. It is my fault. I, alone, will be punished," Black Knife, who had seen two-tens of summers, answered dismally. They had just started up the Spirit Water River for the ten-day paddle upriver to Black Bear Village. The sun had not yet risen above the horizon.

Behind a sand bar in a small lagoon on the western side, along the Spirit Water River, ten-and-six summers old Flying Hawk noticed a canoe with a man and two boys casting a net. They turned around and approached the fishermen.

This time, not taking any chances, Black Knife pulled his bow and confronted the man, who, it turned out, had only seen two-tens of summers himself. He claimed he was the older brother of the boys and was showing them how to cast a net.

Black Knife abducted all three. Despite protests from the young man, Black Knife was convinced he had found the missing fugitives from Long Pine Village. He had them bound and gagged, and started for Black Bear Village as fast as they could paddle. He split his warriors, putting two in the fishing canoe with the two boys, and taking the young man in the war canoe. He never told the captives why they had been taken. He would let Thunder Throat have his pleasures. Had he paid any attention, he would have known the young man looked nothing like the young *man* they had confronted ten days past on the Youghiogheny River.

By the time they made their first camp, Sharp-shinned thought they had made a mistake, but was unable to convince Black Knife. When they camped on the third night, Black Knife slowly concluded that he had, indeed, captured the wrong people. Rather than releasing their captives, Black Knife decided to keep them and present them to Thunder Throat as slaves. He thought three new slaves would be better than returning empty handed.

Thunder Throat's frustration only increased at the blunder, but he had the young man and two boys executed none-the-less.

CHAPTER 10
"BOYS"

It was the day of the Solstice Celebration where the children would compete in games. All the villages of the Monongahela People had contestants in the games, except Black Bear Village. It was the third solstice in a row that no one from Black Bear Village attended.

For the youngest children there was kickball and running games. Anyone ten summers and younger could also compete in spear throwing, bow and arrow shooting, bola throwing, and foot races. Anyone older than ten summers had these choices plus wrestling and club combat.

The ten-summers-old Cass and Pena, known as the hermit *boys* named Acorn and Pecan, would compete in each individual contest.

The bow and arrow contests came first and

were made up of two parts. One was hitting a target at ten, two-tens, and three-tens of paces. The second part was to see who could shoot accurately from the farthest down range. The hermit *boys* placed first and second in each contest.

Next came the spear throwing. Great applause arose from the Monongahela Village people when young Oak, son of beloved War Chief Wolf Master and grandson of the Head Matron, Corn Stalk, stepped to the line. He had placed a close third in the bow and arrow contests.

His spear hit close to the center of the deer's heart painted on the life-sized target at ten paces. He turned and smiled at the cheering crowd. No one else got that close until Pecan, the first of the hermit *boys* to throw, bettered him by the smallest of margins. Finally, Acorn, the second hermit boy, put his spear exactly in the center of the deer's painted heart. The crowd hushed in disbelief.

And on it went, all through the games. The two hermit *boys* placed first and second in every competition with Oak coming in a close third. The exception was the distance foot race.

In a cloud of dust, all the boys and a few girls ran in a bunch as they left the field outside the palisade where the games took place. Nearly a hand of time had passed when the leaders came back into view. Pecan was in first place, Oak in second, Acorn in third, and a fugitive from Long Pine Village named Green Leaf next. As they approached the finish line the leaders were sweating profusely and struggling to keep going. Exhaustion was evident on their young faces. But Green Leaf was barely sweating as he extended his stride and passed all three just before reaching the line. He trotted to a stop, stood tall, and smiled. The three others lunged at the finish line and fell, sprawled on the ground, totally spent.

Oak could not believe he only got one second in all the games that day. He told Acorn and Pecan they would not beat him the next solstice when the competitions would be repeated. They smiled at each other and said, "We will see." They knew they would not be in another competition as boys.

―――――

"IT SEEMS the girls are training well," Corn Stalk said to Chinquapin. The Head Matron was in her resplendent, blue-dyed sleeveless doeskin dress with bead, shell, and quill adornment. A row of stylized corn plants appeared along the mid-calf-length dress just above the fringed hem. Her long, gray-sprinkled black hair was wrapped in a tight bun and held in place with copper pins engraved with corn ears on the flattened ends. Three white heron feathers hung down the back of her head. Her wrists held copper, strung shell, and colored-stone bead bracelets. Moccasins matching her dress and decorated with shells that clicked as she walked adorned her feet. She looked wildly out of place talking to the hermit in his dirty, brown-tanned long-sleeve hunting shirt void of decoration. His leggings were also plain brown buckskin, and his plain moccasins were scuffed and dirty. His hair and most of his face were hidden by a floppy raccoon skin hat.

"Aren't you tired of this charade? Wouldn't you rather move into my lodge, get away from that dreadful shelter you are living in? And for the love of the gods, get out of those filthy hunting clothes?" Corn Stalk pleaded with Chinquapin, once known as Water Mint.

The two did have a legitimate reason to talk. After all, the hermit's *brothers* had bested her grandson to win most of the day's competitions. When others were close to them, the talk was about how athletic the boys all were that day. But in private, the women had things to say to each other.

"No, Head Matron, I am doing very well living out there. No one from Black Bear Village suspects we are anything but hermit fishermen. Besides, no one can hear the girls and me screaming in our nightmares most nights. That is the worst part. None of us can sleep without being haunted by that terrible night in that tunnel. I do not think any of us will ever get over it. Cass, or Acorn, says that the nightmares are a constant reminder to keep her focused on her destiny. She calls it 'Wolf's way of training' her. I cannot believe the strength in that one." She shook her head in disbelief.

"By the way, Tallow—I mean Strong Limb—and I have decided to marry. The traders offer no word of Yarrow. They know of no one in Black Bear Village by that name. We suspect that she never pleased Thunder Throat or Falcon, and they killed her. Ta...Strong Limb says it is time for him to move on. Our souls have become one. It will be secret, of course, for now. The girls seem like they are getting stronger and wiser every day. Cass... Acorn, killed a deer the other day with her bow and Pecan caught a turkey with her bola. They just might have what it takes, and they have only seen ten summers," Chinquapin added, sounding confident.

"Good against eight to ten-summers-old boys is one thing, but Thunder Throat is a whole other story. I hope you realize that and are quite prepared to lose one or both the girls when the time comes. It seems such a senseless sacrifice when so much has already been lost," Corn Stalk said solemnly.

"They have a long way to go, and they know it. You should see them work!" Chinquapin answered. "I better leave you and get my *brothers* upriver. They need to get some clothes on. I am afraid someone will see through the dirt and notice their feminine features. Those breechclouts cover too little. And, after all, we are hermits, and we are not dressed to dance. Enjoy the evening, Head Matron."

CHAPTER II
A MOUNTAIN LION

In the shadows, some two-tens-of-tens of paces in front of her, Pena watched the deer making its way down the trail toward the creek. An eroded ledge bordered the trail as it crossed downslope until it met the small, wooded plain. Looking ahead of the deer for a good ambush point, something did not look right. She studied the ledge and saw a large tree that had fallen. Its trunk still lay partly on the ledge and partly up the slope. The limbs and branches had broken off and lay across the trail. In the time since it had fallen, deer and other animals had woven a trail through the debris. But the trunk had an odd bulge on it. Pena studied the fallen tree trunk for some time without moving. When she was about to signal to Cass about an ambush plan, she saw an ear twitch. That brought the bulge into focus, and she could see that behind the log was a mountain lion, lying in ambush for the deer. The nasal call of a red-bellied woodpecker told Cass that a predator was nearby. The girls had concocted a language of bird calls and practiced until they sounded no different from their wild counterparts.

Cass scanned the trail from above. The deer was looking back toward the woodpecker call. A brown thrasher called, giving Cass a signal to look low for the predator. Finally, she saw the mountain lion and gave a brown thrasher answering call. The lion was intently watching the deer which was taking its time descending the sloping trail. The bird calls were common sounds in the forest and so well executed, neither the big cat nor deer were alarmed.

With all the stealth she could muster, Cass worked her way toward the big predator from behind, moving from the cover of one tree to another. She was able to keep a tree trunk between her and the cat all the way down the hill. The deer found a patch of witch hazel protruding from the rocks along the trail and was busy grazing on the nutritious buds. The cat patiently watched. If it made its move now, the deer would get away. Cass slowly closed the distance, being careful not to step on dry leaves or twigs. She was now closer to the cat than the deer was.

The deer finished her grazing and proceeded down the trail. The cat tensed, crouched in a pouncing position behind the log. In a few more steps the deer would be within reach of fang and claw. The deer kept coming. As the cat prepared to lunge, all its concentration was focused on the deer.

Cass took the final two steps around the tree silently just behind the big cat. She propelled her war club up and over her head and down into the cat's skull with everything she had. It was a desperate move because she had to lay herself out over its body to reach the cat's head. If something had gone wrong, she would have been badly mauled or killed. As it was, she landed sprawled out on the dead cat as it twitched in its death throes. Cass rolled off to the downslope side, came up to her feet, looked at the cat with its dented head and let loose a screeching, red-shouldered hawk's call to tell Pena she had killed the big predator.

At Cass's movement, the startled deer turned and bounded back up the trail. Pena noted the doe was carrying a fawn that would be born soon. The young woman's bow was drawn, but she could not release the arrow. The deer did not seem to notice Pena as she stood rock still by the trail.

"Sister, you scare me! Why did you do that?" Pena asked Cass excitedly when she reached the place where the big cat had been so deftly slain.

"I-I am not s-sure. I just saw that mountain lion with its concentration centered on the deer, and it felt like I could sneak right up on it. I could not believe it worked. But then, when I was right there, I realized I could not reach its head without laying out like I did. I had left my bow up the hill a bit, so I had to do what I did. It was foolish, and I would never do anything like that again." She was literally shaking as the adrenaline coursed through her veins.

"On the other h-hand, I-I sure do f-feel alive! It was an amazing feeling, leaving my feet like that and not knowing the outcome. If I failed, I probably would have died. It is a big cat. Look, my hands are still shaking, and my legs are unsteady." Her tongue was moving faster than her brain could form the words.

"Pena, did the deer not run right past you? You killed it?" Cass asked rapidly, her heart still racing and skin prickling all over.

"Sister deer saved your life, Cass. She deserved to live. There was no way I could take her life after she unknowingly distracted that big cat for you.

She was carrying a fawn, too! Hopefully, she will be a good mother," Pena replied.

Together they skinned the cat. After some discussion, they decided to leave the carcass for the scavengers. They had eaten a bobcat once and decided they did not like cat meat. The pelt, on the other hand, would make a warm wrap and the teeth and claws a gorgeous necklace. And they would need the damaged brain for tanning the beautiful hide.

CHAPTER 12
WATER MINT IS PREGNANT

"Where are Acorn and Pecan?" Oak asked Green Leaf, one of the other boys competing in the Summer Solstice children's games.

"I have not seen them for moons. I think maybe they moved upriver or something. You know their older brother has no use for people. I do not think he liked having those boys in the games two summers past. He just likes to be alone. I guess that is why they live a hermit life. I do not think they belong to any clan," Green Leaf replied.

"Too bad. They really made the games fun last time, even if they did win almost everything. There are three from Black Bear Village this time that look almost dangerous. It would have been fun to watch Acorn and Pecan beat them in every contest," Oak quipped.

"You will just have to beat them yourself, Oak," Green Leaf replied.

"Except the distance run. Nobody can beat you at that," Oak complimented.

As the games proceeded, Oak made first place in every event other than the distance run, which Green Leaf won easily.

"Strong Limb, have you seen the way Thunder Throat is treating those boys over at the Black Bear camp? It is like this is war, and they just lost a major battle. I cannot hear what he is saying, but from the looks of it he is spitting shame on them. And they came in second and third in nearly every event. What is wrong with him? If my war chief treated my future warriors like that, he would not be my war chief for long." Corn Stalk stared across the field with disdain on her face.

"I think there is a lack of happiness in the Black Bear camp, Head Matron. And I suspect it is the same in Black Bear Village. Thunder Throat still has his followers even though he rules by intimidation. I think that Night Owl lives in fear of him and feels powerless to reel him in. On the other hand, he has successfully kept the Haudenosaunee raiders out of the Spirit Water Valley. No one challenges Black Bear Village anymore," Strong Limb observed.

"So, Chinquapin and the girls are happy staying away this time? Those girls seemed to enjoy beating all the boys two summers past. I do miss Chinquapin..." A tear formed in her eye.

"They know it is too dangerous coming into the village when he is around." Tallow nodded almost imperceptibly toward Thunder Throat. "Yes, Wa...I mean, Chinquapin is looking forward to being herself again. And she will need to soon enough. She wanted to tell you herself, but she is not here..."

"What is it?" She peered into Strong Limb's face for the truth. "She is with child?" Corn Stalk asked. He only nodded. "We must find a way to bring her here. I do not want her bearing a child out there all alone. I will think on this. You have lived in secrecy long enough," she said seriously.

"Head Matron, I believe it best we talk no more of this while Black Bears are in our midst. After they have left, I will bring Chinquapin and the girls in to discuss our future options," Strong Limb said quietly.

"You are right of course. But how are the girls handling Chinquapin's pregnancy?" Corn Stalk asked, almost in a whisper.

"So far, they are unaware. They have been

hunting a lot lately. Nearly two moons past, right after the snow melted, Cass killed a mountain lion with her war club! It is quite a story." Strong Limb grinned widely, like a proud uncle.

"Killed a lion? With a girl's club? Why? How?" Corn Stalk was beside herself with worry.

Strong Limb relayed the story as Cass and Pena told him.

"Sounds too dangerous. I would rather they be here competing against the boys, so I could watch and protect them if need be. They have seen but ten-and-two summers. They should not be out wandering the forests alone with dangerous animals and who knows what else out there. You understand they were born to be matrons, not warriors or hermits, don't you?" A tear trickled down her face.

Those girls should be preparing to become clan matrons, not warriors against an unbeatable foe. How, why, did I let it come to this? I must find a way to get them all back in here to make them what they should be and forget this crazy idea of avenging their mother's murder. I cannot let them destroy their lives.

"Head Matron, I hear and understand you. But the girls are beginning to show too many feminine features to bring them into a big crowd like this. The boys would catch on all too quickly that Cass, or rather, Acorn and Pecan are *not* boys.

"You were not there on that dreadful night, and I could only watch from afar. They were right there and feel as they do because of what was burned into their souls. Chinquapin and I are happy in one another's arms, but nearly every night, visions of that night invade her sleep. She still wakes up, shaking in my arms, sobbing, crying, sometimes screaming. It is worse for the girls. I know that ending Thunder Throat's reign of terror is the only thing that will lessen the horrors that haunt their dreams. It is what they want, what they need, what they live for, and what they deserve. Their nightmares will probably not go away then, but at least they will have done what they feel they must. I cannot take that away from them," Strong Limb spoke solemnly. "I should leave your side before someone becomes suspicious. I will bring Chinquapin and the girls in as soon as the Solstice Celebration is over, and everyone leaves."

"My ears hear you, Tallow, but my heart does not. We will talk again," Corn Stalk said quietly, not thinking to use his alias.

———

"CORN STALK IS VERY adamant that she does not

want you dropping a child out here in this hermit's lodge," Tallow said to Water Mint.

"I thought I was to tell her!" Water Mint's angry eyes bore daggers into Tallow's.

"You know Corn Stalk. She looked right into my soul and knew immediately. I could not lie to her when she asked. I have been thinking, perhaps it is time to end our hiding. It has been four sun cycles. I am certain Thunder Throat no longer sends his spies here to see if you have reappeared. He must feel that you are dead or left for somewhere far away. We can move into the village, build our own lodge, and live quietly among the Water Plant Clan without drawing attention to our true identities," he suggested, never making eye contact.

"You want to give up on rebuilding Long Pine Village? How can that be? Have you talked to the others? What do they think of forsaking their past, their ancestors? I do not believe I am hearing this from you! And Thunder Throat will never give up searching for us!" she replied emotionally.

"Of course, I have not given up. I...just...want what is best for our child. Out here, things can happen. We have no protection...you have no protection when I am away. And the girls are out hunting and working every day. You are alone too much. When the time is right, we will go on a war walk against Thunder Throat and defeat him. *Then* we can rebuild Long Pine Village," Tallow replied confidently.

"You have a different vision than the girls do. Cass believes that her destiny is to face Thunder Throat alone, by herself. That is what Wolf told her in her vision, and she believes it will happen somehow," Water Mint replied.

"I understand how she feels, but I cannot let that happen. No warrior, man, or woman can defeat him one-on-one. He is too strong, too athletic, and too smart. No, that cannot happen," Tallow responded with conviction.

"I hear the girls coming now. Go ahead and tell Cass what you just told me," Water Mint said coldly.

CHAPTER 13

RESOLVE

"**R**uffed grouse tonight!" Pena announced as she burst through the door hanging on the back side of their small lodge, holding two birds up to show Tallow and Water Mint, a big smile on her face.

"Don't go taking full credit!" Cass came in behind Pena. "One of those is mine."

"You girls keep us well fed," Tallow winked. "It seems I have taught you well. I take credit for these fine birds."

"Both shot while flying, too, Tallow. It took a few misses before we managed to drop them. Pena got her bird first. She only missed twice, but I missed four before I finally got one. These things are hard. They usually flush from behind a tree," Cass said with great excitement in her voice. "We could have gotten them on the ground with our bolas like we have in the past, but we wanted to find a way to hit them with arrows and did!"

"I know they are hard to hit with an arrow for a fact." Tallow beamed. "I will not say how many I missed before hitting one, but it was more than four. Good work, both of you. There is not an animal in the forest safe with you two out there. You have been careful about where you go, right? No other hunters around, and you keep your eyes open?"

"Yes, elder. We are still learning different bird calls to alert each other. We can nearly carry on a conversation with just bird calls," Cass answered proudly.

"Good idea. And I see you are wearing full coverage dull-colored clothing to blend in with the trees. Good," Water Mint interjected. "Tallow and I must talk to you about some things. Clean those birds and put the meat in that stew pot by the fire. We will talk over our evening meal."

———

"TALLOW HAS duties to perform at the final dance of the Summer Solstice Celebration in the village tonight, so he could not stay for our evening meal," Water Mint told the girls when they returned from bathing in the waterhole up the creek. She did not want the girls to know about the argument she and Tallow had had. "He will be back in a day or two, depending on when the visitors all leave. Please stay off the river until he returns." Her demeanor was serious.

Cass could see that there was more Water Mint wished to discuss. *Was that why Tallow went back to the village?*

"We are happy that you stayed here this year. Your bodies are becoming too feminine to be parading around all those boys and those who have become men this sun cycle. Drawing attention with Thunder Throat around is not the best idea. I wanted to thank you for understanding without an argument," Water Mint began.

Pena quickly answered, "You know we are aware of the *changes* and are quite prepared to be cautious."

"Although watching the boys hang their heads when we beat them at everything is a lot of fun!" Cass quipped, a big smile on her face.

After a long silence, Water Mint spoke. "I took Tallow as my husband nearly two sun cycles past, you recall. We have been secretly married, and it has not been easy because everyone thinks I am a hermit living *somewhere* along the river. To them, I am raising my two brothers. Our parents had died somewhere far from here, and we are refugees. We have no clan, and we live alone. We have been able to carry out this charade for more than four sun cycles now.

"But things are getting ready to change. You two will not be able to pose as boys any longer. And I will make a poor excuse for a hermit fisherman with my belly sticking out to here." Water Mint put her hand out to show how big she would be before the baby came.

"You are having Tallow's child?" Pena asked excitedly.

"Yes, sometime around midwinter, and we are excited about it," Water Mint beamed. At two-tens of sun cycles in age, she was a little old to be having her first child, but that no longer mattered. Tallow was the right man. They slowly fell in love after *that night*, as they referred to it. Tallow had built their hermit lodge in a rock crevice back off the river so that it would be impossible to find unless you knew it was there. After that he provided food and brought gifts from Corn Stalk, Water Mint's great-aunt and Head Matron of the Monongahela People.

Tallow also trained the girls in the making and the use of weapons, as well as tracking and stealth tactics. Eventually reality set in that Tallow's first wife, Yarrow, who had been taken as a slave in the destruction of Long Pine Village, was not coming back. Finally, word came from a trader that she had disrespected her captors too long, and she was put to death.

"Tallow and the Head Matron have discussed it and think that we should move into the village now. Tallow can build us our own lodge, and we can live there quietly. By now Thunder Throat has given up looking for us, and if we use different names, we can just live quietly. Corn Stalk will see to it that suitable husbands are found for both of you. We will belong to the Corn Clan of Mononga-hela Village," Water Mint explained, not sounding too sure of herself.

Cass flushed and started trembling. In a small voice, while shaking her head, she said, "No, no, no. We cannot expose ourselves. H-h-he will n-never g-give up. No, no. We, *I* must fulfill Wolf's directions. I must stop Thunder Throat! You go, I-I will s-s-stay here." Tears formed in her eyes. Pena put her hand on her sister's shoulder, and Water Mint came and hugged her.

"I am so sorry, niece. None of us will go anywhere. We are in this thing together. Some-how, I will make the Head Matron understand. I am so sorry to upset you," Water Mint cried on Cass's shoulder.

Pena joined in for a three-way hug and whispered, "Together, until it is done."

That night, Cass thrashed in her sleep and started screaming. Pena wrapped her arms around her to calm her down, saying softly, "It's all right. I am right here." Water Mint rushed over from her blankets and wrapped herself around the twins.

"It will be all right, Cass. We are all here together," Water Mint soothed her.

"He was here!" Cass cried out. "He reached into me and pulled my stomach out," she cried. She cried like she had not cried in four sun cycles. Every time she closed her eyes, she saw his massive war club slicing through the air toward her head. "He is coming," she sobbed, tears rolling down her face in torrents.

"You are with us. You are safe now, Cass," Water Mint sobbed, her own tears flowing. *You must understand, Corn Stalk. These girls stay here until Thunder Throat is dead. We cannot return to* normal. *There is no* normal *for anyone in that tunnel that night. For the love of the gods, will there ever be peace for us?*

Eventually they all fell into a restless sleep embracing each other. By the time light began to show through the smoke hole, thunderbirds had taken flight and their booming calls rolled through the valley. A couple of fingers of time later, rain started patting against the bark walls of their small lodge. The rain grew in intensity, and even some hail slammed against the walls. Wind started howling and raking through the trees. Occasionally branches and limbs could be heard snapping off and crashing to the ground throughout their surroundings. In a couple hands of time, the downpour slowed to a steady rain that then lasted through the day.

"This will delay the visitors leaving," Pena noted, thinking it could be days before Tallow returned.

"Tracks will be easy to find on the trails," Cass said to no one in particular. She was chipping a sharp edge on a new arrow point with a deer antler. Larger flakes lay scattered on the buckskin she had laid on the floor when she began shaping the arrow point from a fresh chert blank. "Tallow had better stay away until the mud dries up," she said.

"Let's play a string game, just like we used to," Water Mint said out loud.

That night, while the rain continued to fall, the dreams came again. All three clung to each other as they huddled under their elk skin blankets.

———

THREE DAYS PASSED before Tallow came through the door hanging. His moccasins were completely soaked. He wore only a breechclout and was covered with a bear fat and mint mixture to ward off mosquitoes. His hair hung loose. He carried a shoulder bag, his bow, and his quiver. His war club hung from his belt, and he wore a big smile on his face. "I have rice bread and a jar of honey," he said proudly.

"You also have soaking feet, you smell like bear fat, and I have never seen you look so good!" Water Mint beamed.

He looked at the girls and chided, "What have you been doing? I see no fresh deer or turkeys hanging outside."

"We have been waiting for the rain to stop and the trails to dry, so we don't leave tracks. But it appears that did not occur to you," Pena snapped back.

"For your information, I walked up the creek, which is near bank-full of cold, rushing water so I would not leave tracks. My feet and legs are freezing!"

"Well, don't ask Water Mint to warm your blankets, you have already done your work on her!" Cass blurted out, not knowing where her sassy tongue came from.

Tallow looked down into Water Mint's eyes as

she clung tightly to him. She just smiled and shrugged. "So, everyone is happy about it? We are moving to the village?" He looked around, smiling, and getting blank stares in return. He looked questioning into Water Mint's eyes.

"We have had some serious discussions while you were gone fulfilling your duties as an adopted warrior in Monongahela Village. We have concluded that we are Long Pine villagers. More importantly, Wolf himself talked to Cass at the very worst of that terrible night, four sun cycles past. He gave her a mission, and she fully intends to complete that task. She knows she is not ready yet. She also knows that she will know *when* she is ready. Pena understands her role in this as Cass's second. I understand my role is to help them prepare for that time. I must protect her from outside distractions. If we move into the village, the Head Matron will inflict as many clan duties as possible, along with guilt for not performing them. Under that pressure, Cass and Pena will lose their concentration and dedication to the horrible task that lies before them. No, we will stay right here as a hermit family until Cass is ready to face Thunder Throat on her terms," Water Mint boldly told Tallow.

"Come now, think about this. Up until now, we have stayed hidden from the watchful eyes of the

Black Bear. Those eyes have become sleepy and can no longer see the need to capture the three girls who escaped that awful night. We have protected you to the point you no longer need to stay hidden. It is now time to come out into the sunshine and live a normal life. Bury the past and walk a new path. And this thing about Cass facing Thunder Throat. It is pure folly. At best I could muster three-tens of warriors to go on a war walk against his eight-tens. And ten of my warriors would be inexperienced young men. We would be slaughtered before we got anywhere near Thunder Throat. It simply cannot be done. Think about it. The girls will become women in a season or two. It is better to work them into clans where they can marry well and make their ancestors proud of them," Tallow answered back.

"I am to face Thunder Throat alone, Tallow. There will be no war walk. I do not know yet how it will work, but I will face him by myself. And I will defeat him. Wolf told me that. And that will make my ancestors proud," Cass said calmly.

"Cass, you must be realistic. I would not face Thunder Throat with five men. He has killed at least ten-tens of good warriors. What makes you think you could have any chance at all? No, it is time for you to give this notion up. Come to Monongahela, make a home, become a clan matron and someday a head matron. But forget this silly notion that you are or will be a warrior. It cannot happen. To begin with, the laws of our people do not permit women warriors. You will not even find someone willing to give you the tattoos. Your war club is worthless against Thunder Throat, and there is no way possible for you to wield one that would be effective against him." Tallow attempted to speak with authority, but his lack of confidence was evident.

"I know you had this vision when things could not get any worse that night. But have you considered that it was just your brain overriding the horrible things you were witnessing? It is time for you to grow up now and stop fantasizing about something that cannot happen." Tallow tried to use the voice of reason using words Corn Stalk told him to use.

Cass retorted in a calm, confident voice, "Tallow, you and Water Mint have a family now. You should move into the village where your little one will grow and be with other children. I am charged with a dreadful task, and I will see it through. I only ask that Pena be available for me to work with. We must think as one to get this job done. Therefore, we must spend our days together getting stronger, faster, smarter. A plan will come to me someday, and we will make it come true.

Wolf told me this. You do not have to believe it. You do not even have to support me any longer. I am most grateful for what you have taught us. I would ask that you do not identify me to anyone." Her eyes were unflinching as she looked straight into Tallow's.

"I will continue to come into Monongahela Village from time to time, as a boy for now. I will need to trade for obsidian and chert, as well as corn and other food supplies. I, *we,* can provide our own meat, nuts, and many food plants. I bear no hard feelings, in fact I encourage you to take Water Mint into the village, if that is what she wants, to make a new life. But after Thunder Throat is defeated, I expect there will once again be peace, and Long Pine Village can be rebuilt. I believe Water Mint will be the Head Matron if she chooses to take that path. Me staying here and playing the part of a hermit boy, and eventually man is not negotiable. Pena can make up her own mind, as can you, Tallow."

"Do I get to say anything here?" Water Mint asked as Pena walked over and stood next to Cass, locking their fingers together. "I was there with these girls on that awful night. I lived what they did. We are one clan. The Water Plant Clan of Long Pine Village. I know Wolf came to Cass that night. I witnessed it. And I will stand with her and help her see this task to its end. My child will be born in this lodge, and he will learn to be a great warrior, like his father. Let us hope that Wolf comes to Cass with instructions before we are all old and gray.

"Husband, I understand you have responsibilities with the Monongahela and will need to be gone too often. But my bed is here, and you are always welcome in it. I will go to Corn Stalk and make things right with her. But I am staying here with these girls until this is done. I hope you understand, husband, but it can be no other way."

"It looks as though I am outnumbered here. We will find a way to make this work. If I am to be War Chief of Long Pine Village, I better sharpen my own skills," Tallow acquiesced.

CHAPTER 14

PENA KILLS A BEAR

The first hint of a new day brought the slightest gray tinge to the eastern horizon of an otherwise bleak, overcast sky. Pena stood on a substantial limb of a big chestnut tree next to a game trail on the edge of what had once been a planting field for Long Pine Village, where she had been born. She felt a tie to this part of the world and enjoyed hunting here. Cass would be in a tree overlooking a field near the old canoe landing. Deer frequented the old plaza and ruined village site. The new woody growth springing up in the ashes of the old village and fields attracted many deer and more than a few elk.

Pena listened and watched for movement as she looked down from her perch some three times her height above the ground. Deer seldom looked up, making it easier to draw her bow back without alerting the animals. There was only a slight northwest breeze, so she mostly looked to the northwest, west, and southwest. Her scent may give her position away in the southeast and south. She knew her scent was strong because she was in her moon. She and Cass both preferred to go on long hunts while in their moon rather than sit for several days in the small woman's lodge Tallow had built for them.

Four fingers of fresh powder lay over the old, shin-high crusty snow on the forest floor. It was unusual for this much snow so early in the cold moons, but here it was. She had cut a fresh deer trail just about fifty paces south of this tree. The two deer were moving toward the west. The tracks, even in the dark, revealed a doe traveling with last spring's fawn. Hopefully, Cass, moving to her hide, would push them back toward Pena.

Suddenly Pena heard a branch snap to the southeast of her location. *What, I have never seen anyone hunting in this area.* She clung tighter to the tree to make herself invisible. A sound—huffing and heavy footfalls. *A bear, and a big one at that! Up from his winter sleep already? Seems a little early for bears, although I have heard that some male bears do not hibernate at all.* She started to relax. It came snuffing along the deer track, following every turn. But when it got to where Pena had cut the deer trail, it stopped, looked around, and sniffed carefully. Abruptly, the bear veered off the deer track and followed her footsteps right to the tree. She could tell it had caught her scent and showed no fear. By now, it was full light, but the sun would not be seen as it cleared the high hills east of her position on this cloudy day. The bear looked up at her. It sniffed the air and the tree where she had climbed up.

The bear has started climbing! She had no intention of killing a bear this morning—or being killed by one. She was ill-equipped to drag a bear that weighed at least four times what she did to the place where she and Cass hid their canoe under some brush next to the river last evening. First, she waved her arms to try and frighten the beast away, but it kept cautiously climbing. She shouted, "Go bear!" but it kept coming toward her. She had no choice. She drew her bow back, aiming at the bear's snout. Pena let her arrow fly when the bruin was about her body length below her. Just as she released the arrow, the predator bobbed its head slightly and the arrow skidded up the slope of its skull between the eyes. It ripped through the skin just above its brow, slit the skin to the bone up his forehead, and careened off into the brush.

The bear became enraged but took a few heart-beats to recover from the shock while roaring its displeasure. That gave Pena enough time to pull another arrow from her quiver and reload her bow. Now the bear was roaring as it accelerated up the tree. Her next arrow, released just before she was about to jump to another branch with the bear right at her feet, drove deep into its mouth. Panic sounded in its gagged roar, and the big bear let go of the tree with its front paws, trying to get the painful foreign object out of its throat. In the struggle, the bruin lost its grip on the tree with its hind legs and fell.

The bear hit the ground with a big crunch, the shin-deep old snow cushioning its fall somewhat. The bear was rolling around, frantically trying to clear its mouth and throat so rapidly she could not get clean aim for a kill shot. The bear must have driven the sharp chert point through its esophagus and clipped one of the big neck arteries. After a few more heartbeats, it became clear that one arrow was going to end the bear's life. Rich red blood was pumping from the bear's mouth, and the animal was beginning to slow down as it weakened. Finally, the beast rolled onto his side and let out a garbled whine. Blood sprayed from its mouth. She could see the eyes roll back as its hind legs quivered and shook. Then, the great beast was still.

She stood on the limb in disbelief, shaking, knees weak. She stood there deciding if it was safe to come down when another movement caught her eye in the area where the bear had come from. She froze. *This animal makes no noise—it must be a man, a hunter. But who? Is Tallow looking for us? No, he would not come from that direction. Black Bear warrior? Maybe. I cannot let him find me. If he does, from here I might be able to kill him. If I kill him, the Black Bears will know Long Pines are hunting in these woods. They will track me down. What shall I do?* Now she could see him, he was following the bear track but was moving quickly. The man appeared to be alone. He must have heard the commotion. Finally, he got to the place the bear had cut her tracks. He looked over at the bloody snow and the bear, then looked at the tracks and up the tree—at her. She stood proud, bow drawn, ready to release an arrow.

He put up his arms and called, "Don't shoot! I mean no harm. I am only a hunter—after the same quarry it seems."

That voice? It sounds like a touch of Long Pine accent. Could he be one of the children taken in the massacre? Who is he? "Who are you, only a hunter?" she demanded, keeping her arrow aimed at his chest.

"My name is *Bud*," he said nervously, then added, "You are a girl! Who are you?"

"I am Pena, a slave from Monongahela Village. My master sends me out to hunt because I can shoot a bow," she said, trying to sound convincing.

"I don't believe you. First, you are a long way from home. No slave gets that much freedom, no matter how good they are with a bow. Second, no slave is permited to have weapons where I come from. Finally, you do not talk like a slave. You sound like...like one of us. By the gods? Are you...? Could you be one of the missing twins? Bright Moon? Bright Star?" His mind and mouth were running faster than he could put sentences together.

"I have no idea what you're talking about, but I want to come down out of this tree. Put down all your weapons and move back a hundred paces," she ordered.

"I told you..."

"Drop your weapons and move!" she shouted. He obeyed. Once on the ground, she motioned with her hand and called out to him, "All right, you can come back over here." She had her bow loaded, but relaxed, still pointed in his direction.

"So, who are you, and what are you doing out here? Have you been living out here in the forest all this time? You must still be a girl, but you talk like a warrior. I am intrigued," he said with a broad smile on his handsome face.

"It may be more important for me to know who you are," she calmly replied.

"I told you I am Bud, adopted into the Heron Clan of Black Bear Village. My adopted father is Long Tooth, of the Wolf Clan, and my mother is Goldeneye, of the Heron Clan. I am on a hunt to claim my manhood. In my village, I must kill a man or a bear to get into the circle of men. A bear was within my grasp until you killed it. I could kill you, but I do not think Thunder Throat would accept a girl, even if she is an enemy warrior. But maybe your teeth on a necklace?" he said nonchalantly, smiling broadly at her.

"You talk pretty confidently for a boy who has an arrow pointed at his chest," she sarcastically replied.

"I think if you were going to kill me, you would have done it by now. What are you going to do with this bear?"

She did not know, had not had time to think about it. "Do you want it?" she asked as she lowered her bow for the first time.

"It is four days, mostly uphill, to Black Bear Village, five days dragging that bear with help. And six days, with help, downriver to Mononga-hela Village. It is your bear, what is your choice? If you help me drag it to Black Bear Village, I suspect you will become a guest, at least until Thunder Throat determines you are not one of those twins. If you are, I think you would rather have dragged this bear back to your home by yourself." Bud talked freely, his eyes glued to her pretty face.

"Is it normal for your boys to talk poorly about your war chief? And how does an adopted son get to hunt so far away from home without supervision?" She was getting interested—-he was a handsome boy, nearly a man. *I am already a woman, but he does not need to know that—yet. Maybe this boy can be coaxed away from Black Bear Village before he becomes corrupt.*

"There are many who are not adopted who think as I do; that Thunder Throat is an evil war chief. Do you know he has never taken a wife, but has bedded with nearly every woman in our village and every camp in the surrounding region?

"It is only a matter of time until Thunder Throat can field enough warriors to attack Monongahela Village, you know. So, you will probably get to *know* him whether you want to or not," he said bitterly. "I better shut up...I-I have said too much."

"Surely your warriors will stop him, overthrow him someday, will they not?" she sincerely asked.

"No, he is too strong, and has many spies. We

have earned his trust by doing all he requires of us," he answered.

"I know some refugees from Long Pine Village. I have heard talk of a woman named Yarrow who was taken. Is she still there?" she asked, eyes diverted to the west.

"That was six sun cycles past. No. First, Falcon tired of her, then Thunder Throat took her and let other warriors use her, but they could not break her spirit. Finally, he tortured her until she died. He was convinced she would know where Water Mint had taken the Head Matron's daughters." He hung his head as he talked. "It seems I have talked too freely for too long, but something about you..." he tailed off.

"I should do something with this bear. Seriously, you can have it if you like. You could claim it and become a man and would not have to hunt bears, or men, alone anymore," she said lightly.

"I think I would rather come back out here hunting...for you," he smiled. She returned his smile.

"If you help me drag it southwest of here a hand of time or until we hit the river, I will come back here to hunt...to meet you," she said coyly.

She dressed the bear out, offering him some of the still warm heart. They each took a length of hemp rope from their hunting bags, tied a line to each hind leg, and dragged the bear on its back across hill and valley until they got to the river floodplain. He was amazed at her strength. Along the way, they talked more about the troubles in Black Bear Village. She learned that Head Matron Night Owl is afraid of Thunder Throat, as is the rest of the Council, so they do as he says. He can beat, accost, even rape any woman he wishes, and there is never any action taken against him.

She confided that she lives outside of Monongahela Village with a hermit because she secretly wants to be a warrior, is not interested in becoming any man's property, but wants to prove she can fight as well as any man. The hermit has been training her. He is a hermit because he was once a great warrior, grew tired of fighting, and went into reclusion. She thought it best not to mention she had already been in her moon twice.

When they were within hearing range of the canoe, Pena let out an ear-piercing scolding call of a red-shouldered hawk to get her sister's attention. One answered from up the river. When they got closer, she let out a blue jay gathering call and doubled it. Thus, letting Cass know that Pena was not alone. When they got to the river, the canoe was out in the open on the bank with a field-dressed deer carcass in it. A wood thrush called from behind Pena and Bud. They turned to find

Cass standing there less than ten paces away with her bow drawn and an arrow pointed at Bud's heart.

"It's all right, Cass. He is harmless," Pena said quickly.

Cass looked at her in disbelief and, without lowering her bow, said, "How can it be all right? Is he your slave? Are we taking him downriver? Maybe knock him out and dump him overboard? What in the name of all the gods is going on?"

"His name is Bud. Bud this is Cass, my friend I told you about. Bud is of the—"

"He can introduce himself, friend," Cass interrupted, looking him square in the eye, bow still raised.

Bud introduced himself and added, "Your friend here killed *my* bear, and it is too big for one person to drag all this way, so I helped her. Now, I had better get headed back to my camp before they start to wonder where I am. I am sure we will meet again in these woods. Maybe next time I will be a man, and you two will be women."

"Don't go making any plans, boy," Cass said in a warning tone.

"Oh, don't worry about that, she already warned me that no man is in her future. You two look a lot alike, so I am thinking the same goes for you." The confidence was back in his voice. "I will lay as many tracks as I can in this area so that none of my people will think anyone else except me was hunting in this area. Your secret is safe with me." He looked at Pena, "I will see you in two-tens and four days, at your bear tree," he said.

As they guided the overloaded canoe downstream toward Monongahela Village, Cass berated Pena, "How could you? You know nothing of that boy! He is probably one of Thunder Throat's spies! Now you have exposed us, and we are as good as dead! We will probably be attacked before we make it home. Did you even think that by helping you with that bear, he was just learning what he could about you and where you hide your canoe? Now that he has seen both of us together, he knows we are twins, he will put two and two together, and all Black Bear Village will be after us again. How could you? I think your loins got between your eyes and your brain."

"Easy, sister. He told me much more about Black Bear Village than I told him of us. He wanted to tell me. He wants an end to Thunder Throat and his rule. The War Chief has their Head Matron living in fear of him. They are all afraid of him. This Bud can be our spy in Black Bear Village. We can use his information to plan a strategy to get to Thunder Throat. He is one of us, you know. We knew him as Frog, Black Willow's son. It is probably best that we do not say anything to her just yet. She would likely start a war and get the boy killed, and us, too. But I think running into him is good fortune. I trust him."

"I do not! If you think I will let you come back here to hunt in your next moon, you are crazy," Cass said emphatically.

"Oh, I will be back. He will not know I am there until I am convinced no one is with him, but I will be there," Pena said confidently.

"Then I guess I will be watching your back." Cass paddled harder in frustration.

CHAPTER 15
CASS MEETS A BEAR

Pena announced to everyone in their small lodge she was going hunting alone for several days, until her flow started and ended.

Cass knew Pena was going to meet Bud, and also knew she could not stop her. Cass did not want any part of being around when Pena gave herself to Bud, or any man. She decided to stay and help Water Mint with the baby as much as she could.

After a couple days of cleaning a baby's smelly bottom and making him cry because she just did not have *a way* with the child, she decided to take a half-day and hunt by herself. She told Water Mint she would be back before sunset and hoped to have fresh meat. Tallow was due back the next day, and Cass did not want Water Mint to be alone while her husband was in the village. Though it was a warm spring day, it was early in the season, and cold weather could return at any time.

Cass worked her way to the southwest where she knew a fire had gone through at least two-tens of sun cycles past. The hot burn was started by a lightning strike near the end of a prolonged drought. The lightning storm did not even produce any rain, she had been told. After the fire, the first trees to reclaim the burned area were pines. They were now thick and stood about four-tens of hands high.

Where a few of the pines had died, due to over-crowding, elk or deer polishing their antlers, or some other factor, berry bushes, witch hazel, or other shrubs or trees filled the voids. That diversity had attracted many game animals ever since the fire.

As Cass neared the old burn area, her mind uncharacteristically wandered. She thought of her sister and what she might be doing with Bud. At her age of ten-and-five summers, she had never given a boy or man much thought. Her mind was focused on killing one man. All other men played no part in her conscious thought. Further, she could not figure out why Pena would let herself be distracted by a boy when their mission was still not completed.

Was there some magic spell Bud had cast on Pena? Sure, he was handsome, big, strong for his age, and smart. But so what? We must think about Thunder Throat and how to kill him before we can allow any distractions to get in the way. I will need to have a serious talk with her when she gets back!

Is she laying on a blanket with him on top of her? Has he planted a seed in her? How can she let a man touch her after seeing what a man did to their mother? The thought of Bud's hands exploring her sister's ripe, young body sickened her. Yet, she could not chase the image of Pena succumbing to Bud's hardened manhood from her brain.

Suddenly, a movement to her right brought Cass out of her reverie. Something was scurrying up one of the skinny pine trees some three-tens of paces to her right. Her first thought was a porcupine, because of its size and shape. Then, she realized it was a very young bear cub.

Suddenly, a loud growl told her where the mother bear was—at the base of the tree the cub was climbing. The bear did not hesitate when it located Cass. It charged and was moving faster than Cass could pull an arrow from her quiver and draw her bow. A flash thought told Cass that her bow was not even strung. She quickly cursed herself for being distracted in the woods. But she had no more time for contemplating—she needed an escape route right now!

A quick scan told her the only thing she could do was scurry up one of the pine trees and hope it would hold her weight, and the bear would know it would not hold its weight. Cass had no time to pick out the perfect tree, so she started climbing the closest one.

The other thing Cass did not notice while she was distracted with her thoughts about her sister was that the weather was changing. When she left the lodge, the sky had just a few puffy clouds, it was warm, and there was a light southerly breeze. As she hurriedly climbed the tree, she looked up and saw an overcast sky, felt a northwest wind, and declining temperatures.

As Cass climbed the tree, she discovered she had to concentrate on keeping her weight close to the trunk. The few branches sprouting from the trunk were small and broke readily so she could just shimmy upward, squeezing the trunk with her thighs and pulling herself upward with her hands.

When she got about two-tens of hands off the ground, she felt the impact of the mama bear slamming into the tree. The fact that she had to hold on tightly to climb helped her from being jarred from the tree trunk. But now, the bear was trying to climb after her, and she felt the tree begin to lean. That put her own weight off the side of the tree, and the trunk bent sharply.

She looked at the bear. It was determined to get to her. The higher the bear got, the more the tree bent. Then, Cass got close to an adjacent tree and transferred to it. Once again she could center her weight, and the new tree remained straight so she could climb higher.

The bear carefully climbed back to the ground and went after Cass's new tree, growling the whole time. This tree had larger branches near the base. The bear quickly climbed as Cass frantically shimmied higher up the tree. She was now in danger of bending that tree. The bear got about twenty hands off the ground, and only a few hands below Cass. She was able to transfer to yet another tree. The bear pursued her. Suddenly there was a loud cracking noise, and the bear fell to the ground. Now, the sow was furious. It rapidly ascended the tree trunk until about an arm's length below Cass.

Cass put her weight to the side of the tree away from the bear. The supple trunk bent toward Cass's weight. The bear tried to follow Cass, but just as Cass transferred to another tree, the bear was making a desperate attempt to reach her. There was a loud cracking and snapping sound as the tree trunk shattered, and the bear haplessly fell back to the ground. This time, the broken end of the tree trunk dropped like a war club onto the bear's exposed rear leg.

The bear screamed in pain and anger as the jagged end of the heavy tree trunk grazed the inside of its leg, ripping skin and tearing muscle. The bear quickly righted itself and limped to the tree Cass now perched in. It was another pine with a trunk that would support Cass but not Cass and a bear that weighed at least twice what she did. The bear made an attempt to climb, but the effort was just too painful with its wounded leg.

Cass watched the bear slump down at the base of her tree and begin licking its wound. The bear made some sound, and the cub climbed slowly down from its perch and waddled over to its mama. The sow suckled the cub while she waited for Cass to tire and climb back to the ground.

At this time, Cass had a few moments to assess her situation and realized she was in serious trouble. It was getting cooler, and a cold mist began to fill the air. The sharp wind made the misty rain feel like ice. In her shoulder bag, the only extra clothing she had was a spare pair of moccasins. She had no robe or anything to fend off the cold. Her buckskin shirt was beginning to soak through, as were her leggings. She had nothing to cover her hands, which were already sore from all the climbing. She had no hat. With the bear waiting for her, she began to think about what Wolf would have her do. She also realized her arm and leg muscles were rapidly tiring from gripping the trees for so long.

Just when she was about to give up hope, Cass heard the cub whine. She looked down and saw the little bear shivering from head to toe. Even its voice was shaky. Then, the mother moaned and got to its trembling feet. The damaged muscles in the bear's left hind leg must have stiffened because she dragged that leg behind her as she started off in the direction of the ridge crest. Cass knew the other side was steep and rocky. *That sow must have a cave or a den on that side. After she disappears over the crest, I can make my escape.*

Cass now found herself shivering and knew she must get moving. Working her stiff muscles and frozen hands during her slow descent from the tree was torture. Every muscle in her body was stiff from the cold, and her feet and hands were numb. Only by sheer willpower was she able to get to the ground without falling.

When she reached the ground, Cass had to focus her scattered thoughts to find and start on the trail back to the lodge. She knew she had to move fast to get her blood flowing into her extremities, but her cold muscles refused to respond for what seemed like hands of time.

Slowly she made her way back to the trail she had ascended the ridge on. Her feet were like rocks —heavy and inflexible. Gradually, she was able to pick up the pace as her muscles began to respond to use and movement as she started to warm and function. At the same time, she was shivering uncontrollably, just like the little cub. She was soaked to the bone by cold rain, and it felt like her drenched buckskin clothing was keeping the cold against her skin while wicking away any warmth her body was generating. Only her hands felt any warmth. That was because she had them tucked tightly into her armpits.

Her next problem was the lighting. The storm clouds made the sky dark enough, but it seemed it was getting darker. *The sun must be setting, and I am at least two hands of time from the lodge. It will be pitch black soon. I will need to feel my way home. Not sure my body can endure that.*

You will *find your way.* Wolf's voice came to her in a calm and confident way. A surge of energy warmed her lagging muscles as she found her resolve renewed. Stumbling over rocks and deadfalls along the trail, she worked her way down through the forest.

After crashing into many trees and tripping over several rocks, she eventually found herself on leveling ground. She knew she was on the flat above the lodge but had no idea where. With no star or moonlight, she had nothing to orient on. She could not feel the worn trail under her numb, sopping feet.

She stumbled along to her right. Then, a miracle. *I smell wood smoke. Water Mint, you just saved my life!* Cass made her way in the direction of the smoke, knowing she was granted a reprieve. *I wonder if Pena is suffering in this same cold rain. Oh, do not be silly, girl—she has Bud to keep her warm. And I am sure they are engaged in activities that will ensure they have no concerns about the weather. I would rather be here suffering.*

As her mind was wandering, a careless step caused her to trip over a fallen tree limb. She landed on her left shoulder on the steep slope and proceeded to roll down the slope, gaining speed. She tried to spread her legs to slow her momentum, but to little effect. Far down the slope, she careened off a large tree, then another. At last, she rolled to a stop in the rocky bottom of the slot where the lodge was located. She knew where she was but was not sure how many broken bones she had.

Feeling around by her hip she found what felt like the broken stub of her upper leg bone. Closer examination with her numb fingers revealed the broken limb of her bow. Further investigation revealed all of her arrows were also broken. She could not find any serious damage to her body. Using the biggest rock she could find, she pulled herself up to a standing position. She was covered with mud, sticks, and leaves, but apparently nothing was broken, even though she was extremely sore from head to toe.

Cass was ecstatic because she knew she was only a hundred paces from their small lodge. She slogged along the muddy bottom of the slot to where her home was warm and waiting. When she worked her way around a rock wall, she could see the orange glow from the smoke hole. *Water Mint and Fingerling must be asleep.*

Cass announced her presence before she pushed through the double thick elk skin door hanging. Water Mint drowsily responded, then answered jubilantly, "Cass, you're home! I was fearing the worst! I was worried you were hurt and all alone out there someplace. Without Tallow here, I had no way to come searching."

Water Mint got busy building up the fire. When she had the room lit up with the growing flames, she turned and saw the mess that was Cass. "Oh Cass, you are hurt. And you are a muddy mess. What happened?"

"I think I should step outside to get these

muddy clothes off," Cass replied, shivering from head to toe.

"Not until I look at that head of yours!" Water Mint exclaimed.

Cass put her hand up to her head and felt warm, sticky moisture, then looked worriedly toward her aunt.

Soon enough, Water Mint had the small gash cleaned and had Cass hold a compress on it while she sliced her wet, muddy buckskins from her body. Cass had multiple bruises and scrapes, but none that would not heal in short order.

As Cass got out of her ruined clothes and moccasins, she related her day and night to an astonished Water Mint. "So, you escaped the bear by leaning a tree against another tree, then hopped over to the other tree like a squirrel? Unbeliev-able!" Water Mint exclaimed as she poured Cass some more willow bark tea. Cass just shrugged and snuggled a deer skin blanket tighter against her warming flesh. Soon, they both reached their endurance and drifted off to sleep by the fire ring.

CHAPTER 16
BUD BECOMES
RED HAND

Water Mint and Tallow had been as hesitant as Cass at first. But the idea of getting Black Willow's son back was enticing. In the end, they decided that Bud would be more valuable as a Black Bear warrior than as another refugee, another excuse for Thunder Throat to attack Monongahela Village. Still, they pleaded with her not to couple with him. Through the next few moons, the relationship between Pena and Bud blossomed. She found it impossible to keep her promise not to share her blankets with him.

One warm day in the Moon of Growing Corn, they met at the old Long Pine Village canoe landing. His hair had been shaved to a roach on the rear left top of his head and an eagle feather hung alongside his single braid. A fresh heron tattoo adorned each temple. Pena was impressed with his step into manhood. "What is your new name, Great Warrior?" she asked playfully.

He looked away from her. Over the past few moons, he had fallen in love with her, even though their love was forbidden. "The good news is I have become a man. I killed a warrior in a raiding party of some northern band that came up the Gorge River. We had a hunting camp on the Spirit Water near the headwaters and intercepted them as they came down river toward Black Bear Village.

"We opened fire on them with our bows while they paddled downstream. They wore painted faces and carried their bows strung...they were not on a friendly trading run. One of my arrows struck one of their warriors in the neck. He was dead before he knew what hit him. In all we killed six and wounded seven of their party of ten-and-eight warriors.

"We captured one, and Thunder Throat tortured him until he was satisfied the warrior gave all the information he had. Then he was staked to a pole in the plaza, and the people were encouraged to make him sorry he had entered Black Bear territory. It was very gruesome, as you can imagine. Our women gladly carried out Thunder Throat's wishes.

"The result of my kill was that I was invited into the men's lodge, initiated, and given the name *Red Hand*. I know it does not sound terrifying, but it suits me." He looked down and away from her. Quietly, he said, "There is more, and I wish I did not have this part to tell you. Goldeneye has arranged for me to marry a Bear Clan girl named Cherry Blossom right after she goes to the women's lodge for the first time. She has seen ten-and-four summers, so that could be at any time. I do not wish to marry her but have no choice."

"Why, is she too fat or ugly? Is she bitter?" Pena asked, trying to hide her stunned reaction. She had not spent much time thinking about his clan obligations. She only thought what these meetings would be like once Thunder Throat was dead. And maybe then, she and Bud would have a future. *Now he is not even Bud anymore, and I will have to live with the knowledge that he will be sleeping with another woman—his* wife. *It does not seem fair after all I have suffered!*

"No, it is not that. It is just...well-well, it is just that she is...not...um...you," he finally stuttered, looking into her eyes, with hopelessness. She looked away, distance in her eyes. "I swear, I will make her divorce me, outcast me from the Clan! I want to be with you, not her. If I knew a witch, I would have a spell put on her!"

"Stop!" Pena responded. "You have your clan responsibilities. You need, *we* need you to act normally. Everything depends on you acting like you are a dutiful member of the Heron Clan and Black Bear Village. You need to keep me informed about what is going on there. We must put our personal feelings aside for now if we are going to make the future better."

"What about you and your clan obligations? he asked impetuously. "I cannot stand the thought of you with another man!"

"I do not have a clan currently. And if I did, I would do what is needed to make sure that the destiny that is mine and my sister's is fulfilled." She bore her eyes into his so that he would understand how serious she was. "I must be going now. Congratulations on your new name, and your upcoming marriage. I like *Red Hand*...it is dignified, and it suits you. Make her happy. When my business with Cass is over, we can talk about *us* again. For now, I need you to come back here now and again to keep me informed as to Black Bear Village's strength and Thunder Throat's plans. Are we all right? We can remain friends?" She asked these questions softly as she embraced him tenderly. She willed herself to hold back her tears of loss.

He hugged her tightly to him, his nervous

sweat odor almost overwhelming. "I do not want to let you go. It is like this is the end of something. When will you and Cass be finished with your business? And you know, your...our...destiny?" he asked weakly.

"I do not know at this time, but I can promise you that you will know when it is." She buried her face in his chest so he could not see her tears. "Now I must go."

————————

As she slipped quietly into the lodge and slid into her sleeping skins, Cass turned to her and whispered, "So how is everything in the North?"

"Let's go down to the river to talk. I have things I need to tell you, without Water Mint hearing."

The river flowed by quietly while a great horned owl hooted in the distance somewhere across the river. Another answered, somewhat closer. "Bud is now *Red Hand. He* killed a northern raider," Pena started, her voice subdued.

"Finally, a man...at least a bear did not have to die for him, only a man," Cass replied blithely.

"You have never trusted him, have you?" Pena asked irritably.

"No. He is an enemy and a man. Is that so hard

to understand? He could easily set up a trap for you, and you would end up just like..." Cass did not need to finish.

"Do you want to hear what I have to say? Or just insult me until I slit your throat?" Pena snapped.

"All right, what is it?" Cass asked impatiently.

"It seems that Goldeneye, Bu...Red Hand's adopted mother has done her clan duty and arranged for him to marry a girl that has not yet entered the women's lodge. As soon as she comes out, they will be married." Pena looked across the river, unfocused, into the silvery moonlight filtering through the leafy canopy.

Cass watched a tear trace down Pena's cheek. She felt Pena's pain as her own eyes filled with tears.

"Red Hand says he does not want a wife...that he wants to wait for me. He said if he knew a witch, he would have a spell cast upon her. I-I...t-told him h-he had clan duties and must mar-marry her. He m-must m-make everything s-seem normal. He h-has t-to k-keep m-me informed about Bl-Black B-Bear Vill—" Pena turned and hugged her sister while the tears flowed.

Cass hugged her back, massaging her shoulders which were knotted up like a mountain lion ready to pounce on a deer. "It will be all right. As soon as I kill Thunder Throat, you can shove this wife of his off a cliff."

"By then he will have children and have fallen in love with her. I won't be able to ask him to abandon his children," Pena sobbed. "How could I let myself fall in love with him? I have no experience. I don't even know what love is, but I know it hurts as bad as any pain I have ever felt."

How can she say that! After all we have seen, Cass thought as she hugged Pena tighter, her own tears dripping into Pena's hair. She thought she would change the subject. "Who were these northern raiders? Did he name them?"

Pena sniffed and said, "No. Just that they came up the Gorge River from the north, then down the Spirit Water, which those northern people call 'Ohi-yo'."

"I have heard it said that we are related to those northern peoples. If the stories are to be believed, when our people first came up the Spirit River, most did not want to stop and settle in this valley. They kept going north and pushed out the people that lived there. That was many generations past, before our clans came here. They are supposedly very fierce and war-like. People to be avoided, I have heard." Cass talked like she did not believe the stories.

"I do not know if they were once our people or

not, but Red Hand tells me that Thunder Throat has turned back many of their attempts to raid Black Bear Village. He says those northern people are constantly waging bitter wars against one another," Pena chimed in, confirming the rumors Cass had heard. "I think I can sleep now." She got up and headed for the lodge.

Cass followed her but could not sleep. *How can we use Red Hand's marriage against Thunder Throat? Hmm, as a married man he would be considered more trustworthy than a single man. Maybe we can use that? Wait, did she say he would use a witch? A witch... hmm, what if a witch started showing up near the old Long Pine Village site? A maniac like Thunder Throat would consider himself stronger than a witch. Might be able to lure him to fight a witch one-on-one. I need to learn to fight with a war club like no man that ever lived! Tomorrow starts a new day!*

CHAPTER 17

CASS MEETS TRAVELER

When two canoes of five warriors each intercepted Traveler, he had not yet seen the canoe landing outside Monongahela Village, but he knew he was close. After establishing his identity as a friendly trader, one of the canoes broke away while the other escorted him upstream. The big landing came into sight along with many columns of gray smoke rising above the trees on the south side of the Spirit River just upriver from the confluence of the Spirit Water River. He had been to this location many sun cycles past. He wondered if the Head Matron would remember him. She had been a newlywed maiden when he was last in the village.

After formal introductions were completed, Traveler was welcomed with a small feast and learned that Corn Stalk did indeed remember him and asked why he had not returned in all the seasons that passed since his last visit. After sorting out their personal lives, Traveler was shocked when she invited him to share her bed. It was there that he confided the real reason why he was traveling east. He learned that she had, indeed, heard traders mention a yellow-haired boy who was found on a beach in the Lenape lands along the coast of the Great Eastern Ocean. She had no more details.

Corn Stalk also confided in Traveler that she was upset about her niece who was delusional about being a warrior and wanted to go after a strong war chief who would kill her like squashing a cockroach underfoot. She begged him to talk the ten-and-five-summers girl into giving up the notion. He agreed to speak to the young woman, but if she had truly been chosen by Power, it would be impossible to deter her from a destiny set by the gods.

TRAVELER AND CORN STALK were paddling upriver from Monongahela Village in his canoe. They pulled up to a large flat rock, more than a hand of time after the village was out of sight behind them.

They slid the canoe into a small creek and hid the vessel behind another large, flat rock. From the rock, they walked along a deer trail on the creek-bank for a finger of time. Traveler had all his senses on full alert in this odd setting. He was escorting the Head Matron in strange territory. Having something happen to her would jeopardize his mission and his life.

Suddenly he felt a sharp point pressing into his back. "Head Matron, you should not be alone in the woods with an untrustworthy trader," a young female voice said softly, but filled with sarcasm.

"Bright Star, that weapon is not needed! Traveler is a trusted old friend of mine," Corn Stalk said, surprise in her voice.

"Cass awaits in the clearing. And this one may be your trusted friend, but I do not know him. Just making sure no trickery is afoot," Pena said calmly as she withdrew her lance from Traveler's back.

"Greetings, young cautious one," Traveler said, then added, "I am glad I am not your enemy." *I must have walked right past her. My senses are failing me!*

"I am Pena, and I have no clan," she said and stayed behind them.

"I am Traveler, and I have no clan either," he replied in his friendliest voice. She did not answer. Corn Stalk looked down and shook her head in frustration. Traveler noted Red Oak, Corn Stalk's grandson and fine young warrior, standing a few paces behind them with a smile on his face.

In another finger of time, they came to a small clearing. A young lady with a drab hunting shirt, stained buckskin leggings, and high moccasins stood with her back against a tree. A strung elm bow and quiver full of arrows leaned against the tree next to her. Her black hair hung in a single braid halfway down her back. A woman's war club hung on her woven hemp belt, and she was nonchalantly cleaning her fingernails with a small woman's chert knife. Despite being dirty, her facial features showed her beauty. Her eyes had the look of someone far older than ten-and-five summers. When they gathered in a circle, Traveler could see that Pena and Cass shared the same features. *Beauty truly runs in this family. Corn Stalk could easily be their mother.*

Another surprise, as a woman who looked to have seen about two-tens of summers slowly walked into the circle carrying a toddler, a strong warrior following behind her. His bow was strung with a nocked arrow.

"Greetings, trader," the young woman with the child on her hip said. "I am Water Mint, Head Matron of the exiled Water Plant Clan, of the exiled Long Pine Villagers. This is my husband,

Tallow of the Wolf Clan, and my son Fingerling. My nieces here are Cass and Pena. They claim no clan for the time being. I do not know what your purpose is here or how much you have heard of our history. But it is our history, and I will not share it with a stranger. The Head Matron requested that you meet with us for reasons she would not explain. I do not mean to sound unfriendly, but this is a secret place, and we lead a secret life. Please state your business so we can disappear again."

"I am Traveler. I also claim no clan and frankly have no idea what clan I was born into, nor even what people. You come right to the point, Water Mint. I appreciate that. Head Matron Corn Stalk asked me to have a talk with Cass, regarding her vision. I have traveled to many parts of the world and have met many people who have had these kinds of visions. I might be able to help her see the vision's complete meaning."

Cass spoke up, "The vision is clear, and I know what I must do. Right now, I could be doing something to help me prepare for that, but I stand here listening to someone I do not know talk about something only a few people are even supposed to be aware of. I do not feel inclined to talk to you, trader. Unless you have some special weapon that I could use in your canoe."

"Everyone is so friendly in these parts," Traveler quipped. "I may as well have stayed with the Illini. Seriously, your story is spread far down the Spirit River, and all the way to Cahokia, and I assume to many other places as well. In my travels, I have met many strong-willed women warriors who, once they understood me, listened to my advice, and either accomplished their stated goals, or walked away from an impossible situation. I am not here to make you do, or not do, something against your will. I am here only to listen to your side of the story and give you what I can in terms of advice."

"What makes you think you have anything to say that someone else has not already told her?" Tallow said defensively.

"I do not know if I have anything, warrior. But if I do, can she afford not to hear it?" Traveler answered calmly. "I wish to speak with her alone if you would all agree. You can watch, to satisfy your safety concerns, but I need some time with just her. With your permission, Head Matron and Cass?"

"I asked for this meeting, so I am agreeable," Corn Stalk said.

"Cass?" Water Mint asked.

"Keep it short, trader," Cass replied.

Traveler looked into her eyes, seeing the depth

and purpose that resided there. "You seem extremely wise for your age, Cass. I can see it in your eyes."

"What I saw on that night would age anyone. Pena and Water Mint have the same knowledge behind their eyes," she said without emotion.

"But you have the *vision*, and that is there too. The Head Matron asked me to talk you out of the thing you feel you must do. I can see in your eyes that you will not be deterred, nor should you be. Your destiny is to fight this Thunder Throat to the death. You understand that I assume?" he asked in a fatherly voice.

"Of course, I understand that. I have been working toward that for seven sun cycles. There is a lot to learn. If this is all you have to say, I should be getting on with my training." She looked away. "I just wish I knew when I will be ready, when it will be time to face him. I know others are dying, and girls are being raped because I am still not ready. Can you tell me when I will be ready, trader?"

"Only you will know when you are ready. Do not blame yourself for what that man is doing. It is out of your control. You can be working on strengthening and sharpening your wits. You will not overpower this man, but you can be smarter. You cannot be faster, but you can be quicker. You will need to take advantage of any opening he gives you. Did your vision say you would fight with just your hands, or knives, or clubs—any hints?"

"Only that I will face him alone," she answered quietly.

"I hear he has a massive war club that will destroy that toy of yours in one blow. It so happens that I do have a war club fashioned by a Caddo warrior in my things. They make the finest war clubs of anyone I know." He kept his *fatherly* voice.

"You know I killed a mountain lion with this club, do you not? I would not call it a toy. But I do understand that mine is no match for his," she said thoughtfully as she slid her hands along her light-weight club.

"Killed a mountain lion? Do I dare ask how?" he asked, awe in his voice.

"I was able to sneak up on it from behind, using trees for cover until I was right at its feet. The big cat was concentrating on a deer it was about to pounce on. I laid out from just above it and drove my club down into its skull. The lion was dead before it knew I was there," she said nonchalantly.

"I believe there is more to you than meets the eye," he said cautiously.

"I have a few furs, but not much else to give you for your club, and I want to see it," she said.

Then added shyly, "I could lay with you for it. I am a woman now." She looked away as she said that.

"I appreciate the offer, but that will not be necessary. I just want you to have the best chance. I like you, and the reason you are doing this thing could not be more honest and honorable. So, in your vision, Wolf only said that you must face Thunder Throat alone? No details on how you would make that happen?"

"I keep waiting for a sign," she replied.

"It will come when you are ready," he said confidently. "In the meantime, practice with your weapons and your mind. Train your mind to think faster than anyone else. Practice catching small animals with just your hands. Learn to avoid being bitten by a rattlesnake as you handle it. You can move faster than a snake if you are not afraid and think fast enough. I advise you to practice with nonpoisonous snakes first. Learn to catch chipmunks and squirrels without being bitten. Then move up to rabbits, skunks, and raccoons. Hawks are very tricky, but it can be done. Master all these things, and no man will be quicker. At the same time, practice playing mind games with other people. Thunder Throat's weakness will lie in his arrogance and overconfidence. Quick strikes and retreats will frustrate him to the point where he will make a mistake and give you an opening to do some real damage. You must be ready for that. Do you follow what I am saying?"

"I do! I am glad you came to talk to me. I feel better already," she answered enthusiastically.

"Good. Also, always keep eye contact with your enemy. His eyes will betray his next move. He must calculate where to strike. By watching his eyes, you will know what he is thinking. Oh, and your endurance will be tested more than words can describe. Staying away from that massive war club will require constant and quick movements. Never give him an easy target.

"Now I need to convince the Head Matron that you could not be deterred from your destiny. I think I can convince her that I could see it in your eyes. Anyone can see that. I have seen dreamers kept by great chiefs who do not have the look that lives in your eyes. Let me ask you this, what is your plan for after you defeat Thunder Throat?" he asked seriously.

"Plan? My focus is on him. I have no plan for after, and probably should not make one. There are better odds that I will have no future after meeting him," she replied just as seriously.

"You show wisdom beyond your years, Cass, or is it Bright Moon?" Traveler said softly.

"That name died in a tunnel seven sun cycles past, and no longer applies to me. I am Cass," she said sternly. He nodded, then signaled for the others to join them. Red Oak had stayed back with the canoe to watch the trail.

When all had gathered around them, Traveler looked into Corn Stalk's eyes and said, "I have listened to Cass's words and studied her eyes."

Corn Stalk could see that even Traveler had been convinced of her story. *How could someone of his experience and knowledge be swayed into letting this child do this thing? Her life is forfeit. I can only hope that Bright Star will not be sacrificed as well.*

Traveler continued, "I have known people who have accomplished what would seem impossible. Cass here, in my opinion, can do what she says she must, though she is not ready yet." Now he looked to Tallow. "She will need continued help in training with her weapons and her ability to read her adversary. I have given her some suggestions, and I have a Caddoan war club, for which I am willing to trade her woman's club. I trust you can teach her how to use it." He turned to Pena. "Pena, you need to work with her in developing quickness of hands and mind. Make her life a challenge. Everything should be difficult until her mind is sharper than a newly chipped obsidian blade. Water Mint, Tallow, Corn Stalk? Do you all understand? Without your unfailing support, she will fail. With it, she at least has some chance."

LATER THAT NIGHT after the evening meal, Corn Stalk and Traveler walked together through the plaza. "So...do you really think she has a chance? Or did she win you over with her charm and beauty?" Corn Stalk asked in a serious tone.

"I would have tried to bring her to her senses if I thought otherwise. I have seen that look she carries in her eyes only a few times—and it was in people who accomplished similar things. I know your people do not think much of female warriors, but a few have been very accomplished. Cass has that *something* nobody can explain that sets her apart. Only people who have claimed to have been visited by real spirits have that. And they do accomplish the impossible. By the time she faces this Thunder Throat, he will be older and have lost a fraction of his edge. If she can capitalize on that and uses his arrogance against him, he will make mistakes, and she will come out the victor. Yes, she can do it," he answered just as seriously.

"That is an awful lot of 'ifs.' I pray you are correct. I hate to see this family suffer another loss," she said remorsefully.

He looked at her sorrowfully and said, "Please do not expect Cass to fall in line with clan responsibilities. Her destiny is outside the clan. Pena, on the other hand, will be all about clan responsibility when this is all said and done. She wears the clan maiden mantle in her eyes. She is a reluctant party to this whole revenge thing. She will do what Cass asks of her. She feels she must. But she wants it over. I think you can count on her as the Head Matron of Long Pine Village someday. But Cass, she is different. She belongs to the gods now and has ever since that horrible night when Long Pine Village was destroyed. You must let her follow her destiny."

"You are saying she is already lost? Bright Moon will never return?" she asked as a tear trickled down her cheek.

"I will be surprised if she even stays in this region. She has no plans and will probably become a wanderer like me. The trader life is one I would not trade for the seat of the Great Sun in Cahokia," he said confidently.

"Have you poisoned her mind about clan responsibility, trader?" she asked as she looked toward the setting sun.

"I only asked her what her plans are when this task is completed. She said she did not think it wise to make plans for a tomorrow that may not come," he answered calmly.

"What will become of her, Traveler?" she

asked, her voice breaking as tears flowed down her cheeks.

"Only time will tell," he answered as he took her into his arms. "I am not cursed with being able to see the future, Corn Stalk. But please have faith in her. She is wise enough to do the right thing."

"Yes, but you have cursed me by encouraging a girl who, by our customs, is my granddaughter, to die at the hands of a monster!" Corn Stalk felt she was losing her composure.

He gently massaged her tense shoulders and said seriously, "I have no power over any gods, Corn Stalk. Cass was most certainly visited by a powerful spirit. None of us mortals are in a position to question the motives or actions of such powerful entities. We can only let them use us as they see fit. If they have entrusted the ending of an evil man's reign of terror to Cass, then we can only help in any way we are able." *I cannot believe I am saying these things I have never believed myself, but what if I am wrong and gods truly are at work here? I should leave them to their work. If Cass says she was visited by a spirit, am I anyone to deny her? No one can doubt that she is a special one!*

"Of course, you are right. The bones are already shaken and tossed onto the blanket. Only fate knows their meaning," she sniffled. "Look at me, acting like a child instead of the Head Matron of a strong and respected People!"

"You are allowed to be a human being now and again, Head Matron. Otherwise, you would not have me by your side to talk to. I am not good with clan responsibility, as you know, but I think I am a good judge of character," he said in an attempt to reassure her.

"Yes, I know." She smiled. "Shall we go down to the sweat lodge?" Her wink was barely visible in the first rays of moonlight.

"I cannot refuse a request from the Head Matron."

CHAPTER 18
FIGHTING MEN

Cass moved stealthily down over the hill toward the flat ground that used to be a Long Pine Village planting field. After seven and a half sun cycles, feral corn and bean plants could still be found among the weeds and tree sprouts. There was even an occasional rotted squash gourd laying here and there. But she was here following a big buck deer. Her plan was to get close enough to kill it with the war club she had acquired from Traveler.

The day was cool, but not cold. The fall equinox had just passed but freezing weather had not yet arrived. Some of the trees, shrubs, and grasses were shifting to autumn colors, and a recent rain allowed for easy tracking.

Cass had left Pena with Water Mint this time. *I*

would rather paddle upriver for six days than go into our women's wigwam when I am going into my moon. Hunting in our old homeland is more relaxing than sitting there in that dreary hut making baskets, mats, or even arrow points. She had hidden her canoe under some overhanging brush on the river bank and traveled far east and uphill away from the old village site to look for deer tracks.

She followed the track in an arc that took it back to the wooded hillside where she stopped to study the situation. From her higher vantage point, a movement caught her eye in the distance. Soon, she could see it was two men, and the clothes they wore were the style of Black Bear Village warriors.

She watched from behind a large chinquapin. They appeared to be following a track. *Must be hunting. I have not seen anyone except Red Hand in this area for three sun cycles.* The two men were looking ahead of their position and only communicating in simple hand signals. Finally, one pointed first in one direction in a circular motion, indicating that the other man should move around to an ambush point. Then he pointed at himself and a circle around the other direction. His path would take him close to her. She foolishly decided to wait and watch the drama play out.

The one moved out circling to the north and

west. The other waited a finger of time before starting to the south and east, toward her. The one moving north, and west was no longer visible and the one coming her way was getting closer.

Suddenly a big buck came bounding by with its tail laying over its back, flashing white for all the deer world to see. The deer's path took it within range of the hunter coming his way, and he put an arrow into its side as it ran by. After jerking at the arrow's impact, the deer ran straight up the hill toward Cass. She froze, ready to draw her nocked arrow back and let it fly if the warrior got too close. The deer staggered just past her hiding place and collapsed. The hunter was following a blood trail that would lead right to her, and now she could go nowhere without being seen.

The hunter followed the deer's blood that led within a few paces of her. He spotted the downed deer and started cautiously for it. He held his bow with a nocked arrow at the ready. She let him pass, then aimed her arrow at his neck and said, "Greetings, hunter."

He whirled, looking for a target for his arrow. She said calmly, "I would drop that bow if I were you." Her arrow had him centered, and he knew it.

A split second of indecision, and he decided to try to wound her. *The girl will panic and freeze. I will quickly have the advantage. Then I will see if she puts up a worthy fight as I take her.* As soon as he moved the point of his arrow in her direction, hers drove through his chest. He collapsed, sucking for air.

"I told you," she said. He quivered and stopped moving. She looked for the other hunter, who by now had figured out what had happened. She moved back to her chinquapin and caught him glancing around a tree, almost in bow range.

"What will you do?" she yelled. "I see you, and you know where I am. Will you run and live, or try to avenge your friend's unfortunate accident?"

"I think it was no accident!" he yelled back. "You saw an opportunity and ambushed him. And what is a girl doing out here so far from a village?"

"That is not what happened! I told him to put down his bow. He thought he was faster and smarter than me. He tried to shoot me. I had no choice but to defend myself," she yelled back to him.

"I think I shall take you back to Thunder Throat. I expect he may want to question you—in his special way!"

"All right then, come and get me!" she called his bluff.

"Big talker, eh? Care to find out if you can fight without that bow in your hands?" he chided.

"I have a club that works very well. Care to test it?" she chided back.

"Love to, little girl. Who are you, anyway?" he questioned.

"I am known as 'Cass.' I have no clan or village. I live alone in the forest," she answered boldly. "Lay your bow and quiver on the ground where I can see it and walk away from it. When I see that you are clear, I will set mine down, too."

"Do you think I am as crazy as Bear Dog? When I drop mine, you drop yours at the same time," he yelled back.

"I will set mine against this tree. I will not drop it because I plan to use it in the future. See, I set it right here. Now you do the same," she challenged. *I must be crazy. I just challenged a seasoned warrior to a club fight. I guess we will see how much I have learned.*

He did the same. They both cautiously backed away from their weapons. She unhooked her club from her waist belt and stood in a small clearing a few steps away. He approached cautiously, club in one hand, obsidian knife in the other. She pulled her hafted chert knife from its sheath. When he was three-tens of steps away, he said, "Get farther away from your bow."

Looking him in the eyes, she said, "That clearing," as she nodded to a patch of grass with no tree sprouts. He looked closely at her and said, "You're nothing but a girl! How about we just play in the grass. If you impress me with a good fight, I will go back and tell Thunder Throat that the dead man fell on his own arrow." He had a gleam in his eye and bulge in his breechclout.

"Funny," she said coldly.

Without warning he came straight after her, drawing his war club back and sticking his knife out in front of him. She easily sidestepped his swing and slapped him on the buttocks with her club as he went by. He wheeled, fury showing in his face. He came again, feinting one way, and swinging back the other. She noted his feint, pulled back, and brought her club down hard on his forearm on the side he held his knife. She felt the bones break as he shrieked in pain. His knife fell harmlessly to the ground. He back swung his club and barely connected with her hunting shirt just below her breast. It hurt. A sharpened lug at the tip of his club sliced through her shirt and grazed her skin just below her breast.

She quickly circled around him, looking for an opening. She faked a swing toward his injured arm, and he reacted by swinging his club in that direction. As his club whirred through the air, she twirled hers around and connected squarely with his elbow. Again, he shrieked in pain, and his club dangled on its thong from his numb wrist.

He stood, looking dumbfounded. She could see

the disbelief in his eyes. He had been defeated, easily, by a mere girl. He had no defense other than his feet. He frantically tried to kick her as she studied him. When his leg came up at her war club, she twirled down and around, then drove her club into the side of the knee of the leg he was standing on. He went down, whimpering.

She knelt by his quivering head. "Tell me, warrior. How does it go in Black Bear Village? Are all the warriors as weak as you? Are the people ready to be rid of Thunder Throat?" she asked, scorn in her voice.

"He will find you, and after he is finished exercising his manhood in you, he will cut you one piece at a time until you are a pile of refuse. Then he will eat your heart. You are a miserable witch. He does not like witches. Your death in Black Bear Village Plaza will be talked about for generations. Ha-ha," he moaned.

"So, you do not wish to start this all over? Just run away when I first called you out. What is your name?" she asked coolly.

"I am Goshawk, younger brother of Falcon of the Hawk Clan," he said proudly, wincing through the pain. "And I would have been more cautious, but I still would have fought you, worm shit," he replied as harshly as he could muster.

"Well, I tried to get you to come to your senses.

You should know better than to tangle with a woman in her moon!" She pulled her loincloth aside so he could see the blood-soaked moss padding. His eyes bugged out, and he started to mutter something. She cocked her club back, swung, and crushed his skull. As soon as his body stopped twitching, a wolf howl echoed through the valley. Cass smiled. She collected all their weapons.

Then, she dragged both bodies to the shallow water along the riverbank, sliced their stomachs open and gutted them, letting their entrails flow downriver to feed fish and turtles. Then she filled their body cavities with creek rocks, crudely sewed them back shut, and shoved them into a deep pool. Then, she went back and dressed the deer and dragged it to her canoe over the tracks where she had dragged the men. When she was finished, only the deer's entrails along with some bloody leaves and grass remained. Coyotes would track up the muddy ground fighting over the deer's entrails. And the imminent rain promised to wash any left-over blood away.

Two hands of time later, the sun's dim light, blocked by the encroaching storm, darkened as it slid below the western hills. Now that the equinox had passed, the days were rapidly getting shorter. By the faint light of the darkening sky, Cass paddled to the west bank to camp for the night. Just as she slid to a stop on a gravelly bank, a cold mist started to fall from the gray sky. She hastily threw together a small wigwam and built a fire with the driest wood she could find.

Cass decided to skin the deer and butcher it so she could protect it from the rain. She cut the legs off and hollowed out the skull. Next, she used her war club to break the skull apart, leaving a piece of bone connecting the antlers, which she tossed into her canoe. Then she scattered what was left of the head and legs far-and-wide, many paces away from her campsite. She hoped those parts would satisfy any coyotes and wolves in the area.

Over her small fire, she cooked some back-strap meat as she thought about her day. She had killed her first two men and given it no more thought than killing a deer, maybe less. *At ten-and-six summers, I have truly become a cold-blooded mankiller. I had envisioned that the only man I would ever kill would be Thunder Throat. I once believed that! What a child I was. I will never get to him without killing others. Red Hand talks about how many truly hate him, but these two were clearly his supporters. I hope I am never forced to kill a woman. That would be hard. Maybe when this is over, I will learn not to hate men so much. But I will always hate men who abuse women. Wolf, I hope this whole thing is over soon.* A wolf howled somewhere in the forest to the west.

She would be home in four more days. Her blood would have stopped flowing by then. She decided to cut up what meat she could eat in the next four days and leave the rest for the wolves and coyotes because she had touched and contaminated the meat while she was in her moon. Just then, she felt more akin to the scavengers than human beings.

She always preferred to go out on these private hunts rather than use the moon wigwam Tallow had built for them. *Poor Tallow. Imagine what it must be like living with three women. One or another was in her moon at just about any given time. Before he built the wigwam, he was able to spend very few nights in his own lodge. Now that Water Mint had two little ones hanging on her, how do they ever find time for each other?*

———

SHE ARRIVED BACK at their little lodge late on the fifth day after her camp in the rain. The growing family was beginning to outgrow the small lodge that Tallow had built hidden in the rock crevasse not far from the Monongahela River. It was built as temporary accommodation for the young girls and their aunt so they could live in seclusion, away from prying eyes and ears. It had now become a permanent home for four adults and two small children. They were all anxious for Cass to have a dream that would put an end to this exile. They, and more than three-tens of other refugees from Long Pine Village, were anxious to rebuild on the old village site.

Cass ducked through the door covering carrying three bows, three quivers, three war clubs, and her big bag with all her other belongings, including a fresh deer skin and set of antlers. Everyone looked at her slack-jawed. "Long story, I will share it over some of that good smelling stew," she said to everyone.

She relayed her story, showing no remorse for taking two human lives. Water Mint asked, "Can you really kill men so callously?"

"I am sorry, aunt, I thought it was self-defense when men are trying to kill or harm you," Cass replied with granite in her voice.

"It is, I just expect you to feel some emotion, maybe some remorse for having to do it," Water Mint answered.

"And how much remorse would those Black Bear hunters have shown after they raped and dragged me back to Thunder Throat?" Cass came back quickly with the same hard voice.

Changing the subject, Tallow interjected, "From the sounds of it, your war club training is paying off. Your description shows that you recognized his feint, and you knew when he was truly swinging at you with intent to harm."

"I think so, uncle. And either he was too arrogant, or too stupid to recognize that I was going to hurt him. It almost seemed too easy. I know Thunder Throat won't be *that* easy," Cass said smoothly, like they were talking about shaping a clay pipe.

"Is there any chance that others will find evidence at your kill site and be able to track you here? Are you certain that no other Black Bears were in the area? And what is this? You were wounded!" Pena asked pensively, pointing to the bloody slit in Cass's hunting shirt. *It could have been Red Hand out there!* She kept that thought to herself.

"It is just a scratch from his war club—see it has a chert blade mounted in the end. It bled a little. I put a slippery elm poultice on it, and it is healing fine. I saw or heard no signs of others, and the heavy rain that night would have washed away the drag marks, footprints, and all the blood. I collected their weapons and picked up everything else they dropped at the site. No one will ever find their bodies."

CHAPTER 19
A PLAN FORMS

"This was the first time I have seen anyone except Red Hand near the old Long Pine Village area. They will probably send someone out looking for them when these two do not return to Black Bear Village. We should probably stay away for a while," Cass said casually. "But the one hunter I talked to the most said something that I have been thinking about coming downriver. He called me 'a miserable witch.' I have pondered about using 'witches' to draw Thunder Throat out from time to time over the past two sun cycles. I think we could use that..." Cass was interrupted by Tallow.

"Yes!" he said excitedly. "If Thunder Throat thinks there is a witch in the forest, he will try to eradicate it. More than likely, he will think it is you and will meet your challenge head on. You might be onto something, Cass."

"I was thinking along Water Mint's line that I want to kill only when necessary—like six days past. What if we make up two identical costumes of...maybe a crow feather cape and a brightly colored mask? Then go out into the forest west of Black Bear Village and isolate single hunters, confront them and with swift club action, break a knee? We would only do this with hunters or warriors loyal to Thunder Throat, as identified by Red Hand. Pena, do you think Red Hand could and would do that for us?" Cass was coming up with details as she spoke. Saying it out loud seemed to ignite her imagination.

"I think he would be more than happy to protect those not loyal to Thunder Throat, while taking the ones loyal to him out of fighting condition. My moon is as predictable as granite is hard. I will leave in four days. I am to meet Red Hand there at our secret location on the tenth day from today. I will ask him for some names and descriptions as well as places they like to hunt," Pena mused, her head spinning in different directions.

"This sounds like a good idea, Cass. But it also sounds incredibly dangerous. Are you sure you are ready to face him?" Water Mint questioned.

"Fingling want fight!" two sun cycles-old Fingerling piped up.

"One day, son, one day." Water Mint hoped for a period of peace while her son was of fighting age.

"Your plan is brilliant, Cass. But it must be carried out perfectly. At no time can anyone see your costumes besides Black Bear warriors who are loyal to Thunder Throat. What's more, you will need to ensure that none of them sees both of you close to each other. A witch who can be two places at once is perfect. Of course, a man like Thunder Throat does not admit to believing in witches. When his men become frightened, he will take matters into his own hands. Cass, I think you have had your vision!" Tallow's voice was full of enthusiasm.

WHEN PENA RETURNED from her hunt, Cass had already caught and skinned thirty crows and ten cardinals. Their face masks would be made of cardinal skins with the feathers out to contrast sharply with their black crow skin capes. Tanning and sewing the fragile bird skins was tedious, but with Water Mint's help, Cass was making good progress with their witch costumes.

As soon as Pena came through the door hanging, Cass could see something was wrong. "What is it, sister? What happened?" Cass asked sincerely. Water Mint, who had just gotten Fingerling to settle into a rare midday nap and was breast-feeding Dewdrop looked on with concern.

"Nothing happened," Pena said dejectedly. "And it never will happen again. Red Hand's wife, Cherry Blossom, is with child. I told myself that I knew this would happen, that Red Hand would never truly be mine. But my heart would not listen. I could not bring myself to couple with him this time. It would not be fair to any of them or me. I told him that I cannot be a second wife. It is just not in me. As long as she was some stranger, it did not bother me that he was married. But now, with a baby involved, I just cannot do it. I told him we can remain friends, and we still need his information, so we will meet again next moon.

"In the meantime, Cass, yes, I did get some names, descriptions, and their favorite hunting areas. *Your* plan can move forward. Red Hand thinks it will work, though it may take some time. Although, with the disappearance of two hunters in the vicinity of the old Long Pine Village, the subject of witches or ghosts, has already been brought up in Black Bear Village. Thunder Throat will suspect a trick before he believes any witch stories. We will need to be ready for him to send many warriors to trap whoever is maiming his followers."

"As usual, caution will be our guide," Cass replied quietly, then added, "There will come a time when you and Red Hand can be together." She did not even look up—she was concentrating on her fine stitchery.

"How can you know that? I see no way for it to happen," Pena snapped.

"I do not know. It just came out of my mouth! I was not even thinking about that." Cass had a bewildered look on her face.

"Sometimes I wonder about you, sister," Pena said bluntly.

"This whole thing is bigger than we know," Water Mint said softly. "Cass has more than revenge working for her, I think."

CHAPTER 20
WITCHES

Cass and Pena patiently watched the camp of eight hunters. One was Skullbreaker, an ardent follower of Thunder Throat, and clearly the leader of the group. The male laughter and loud talk echoed through the trees, but they were too far away for the young women to make out many words. In the morning, the hunters would no doubt split up and follow the game trails in search of fall deer, bucks in rut probably. Cass and Pena already knew which trails the bigger bucks had been using to mark their territory with scrapes and rubs. They had been carefully scouting the area for several days and went into hiding when the Black Bear Hunters parked their canoes. Skullbreaker would claim the most aggressive buck, as would be his nature, according to what Red Hand had told Pena.

The sisters huddled together under a single elk hide blanket to share their warmth in their cold camp. It was cold enough to see one's breath, but no frost had formed by early morning when the hunters stirred and began moving around. Skull-breaker headed right in their direction to relieve himself. First, he untied the thongs holding up his breechclout, put his hand against a tree, pulled down his breechclout with the other hand, and let out his water right in their direction, a cloud of steam rising around him. The young women held their breaths so their exhalations would not betray their location. He re-secured his breechclout and started back toward camp, stopped, dropped his breechclout again, squatted, and defecated. Another cloud of steam rose in the still morning air. The young women, who had now seen ten-and-seven summers, looked at each other and laughed silently.

Finally, the group of hunters split up in pairs and fanned out across the forest in the general direction of the river which ran toward the south-west and was about two hands of time at a slow walk from the campsite. The hunters would return to the lean-to after their day of hunting for the next few nights, depending on how successful they were. Each one said a prayer to a small bundle tied around his neck before leaving the camp.

At a safe distance, Cass followed Skullbreaker and another man she assumed was Buckthorn. Pena followed the one named Three Shots and his partner Fast Feet. High Hawk and Drum Wing went almost straight north, and Red Hand guided Two Hearts toward the northeast. Red Hand wanted to keep Two Hearts away from the *witches*.

After a hand of time, Skullbreaker and Buckthorn found a fresh track. The deer they were following left a circle of freshly pawed up ground. Near the center of the circle was a wet spot. Skullbreaker bent down and confirmed it was fresh deer urine by smelling it. Near it was a small tree with the bark shredded off on one side from about knee-high to almost waist high. A low hanging overhead branch had been broken off. He put his finger to his lips to indicate silence. He then motioned for Buckthorn to circle around to the north and west to cut the deer off before it got to the river. Skullbreaker would follow the trail, stalking the deer.

Through the scrubby brush and tall grasses of an abandoned Long Pine planting field, Skullbreaker silently stalked the deer. He stopped and slowly studied the trail in front of him. About three tens-of-tens paces in front of him was a stand of taller trees on a raised hill. The deer seemed to be headed in that direction. Suddenly the wide-antlered buck bounded onto the trail that led toward those taller trees. Its tail waved over its back, signaling it was running from danger. *Curses, Buckthorn, where are you? He must have spooked my deer. I will deal with him later!* Just before the deer entered the trees it stopped and looked back, slowly lowering its tail. The deer then veered into a copse of smaller trees to hide. Skullbreaker smiled. *You are mine!*

Just as a plan for stalking the buck was formulating in his mind, a person stepped out onto the trail less than ten paces in front of him, pinning him with a drawn arrow. The figure was dressed in a crow feather cape and a bright red mask of cardinal feathers. The black and red arrow with an obsidian point looked menacing. "Greetings, warrior," a scratchy female voice calmly addressed him. "Your days of hunting in my forest are finished."

"Your forest? Ha-ha. I think there are some who would dispute that claim," he snapped back, distaste in his voice.

"Let them come see me, and we will talk about it. In the meantime, you can drop your bow," she replied confidently.

"Why would I do that? I think I will hold it

until your strength fails, then I will see how moist your woman hole is on this cool day," he said with scorn in his voice. His bow and nocked arrow were pointed roughly in her direction but not drawn.

She changed her aiming point slightly and released her arrow. Stunned at the release of her arrow, he hesitated. It slammed into his bow just above his hand. The upper arm of his bow snapped, the impact stinging his left hand and causing him to drop his broken bow. His arrow fell harmlessly to the ground. He yelled out angrily at the stinging pain in his left hand. When he focused back on where the mysterious woman had been, she had vanished without a sound. Stunned, he saw movement by his leg just before a war club drove into his left knee. The sound of his kneecap shattering echoed for several paces around the impact. He fell to the ground, clutching his broken knee and calling out for Buckthorn.

Calmly, the woman in the crow feather cape and cardinal feather mask spoke. "As I said, you are finished hunting in my forest. You can tell your friends that they are finished here as well. Although, there is one I think deserves the same treatment I gave you. Buckthorn will be here soon. He can help you back to your camp. Load up your canoes and do not come back here—ever." With that, she turned and was gone.

THREE SHOTS STOOD and watched the deer bound away through the scrubby brush. Suddenly something crashed into his right knee, dropping him in his tracks. He screamed in pain as he was falling. He landed on his bow, snapping the arrow shaft.

"You are finished hunting in my forest, warrior," a calm, confident, scratchy female voice said. In front of him, through blurry eyes he saw a black cape and a red mask. "Fast Feet will hear you and will come and help you back to your camp. Gather your things and carry them to your canoes. Leave this forest and do not come back—ever!" She turned and was gone.

"HOW MANY TIMES must I tell you fools, there are no witches!" shouted Thunder Throat. His voice could be heard throughout Black Bear Village from inside the Warrior Society's Lodge. "These are people trying to trick you into thinking they are witches."

"But War Chief, you know me, I do not fall for tricks. I am telling you she exploded my bow simply by pointing at it. She moved with speed and stealth no woman possesses. And added to that, she ambushed Three Shots at almost the same time she ambushed me. We were farther apart than a man can run on flat ground in two hands of time. No woman could do that. It must be a witch." Skullbreaker spoke with his mouth clenched in pain. He panted after making his short remarks, his eyes half-lidded. His knee, after four days, was swollen and turning black. His leg would no doubt need to be removed, just like Three Shots was going through at that very moment.

"Did you consider that there are two of them, and they are trying to scare us out of that part of the forest?" Thunder Throat bellowed. "Did it dawn on you that these are our long-lost twins from Long Pine Village, that they are playing some revenge game? Their aunt is out there somewhere too, no doubt! What fools—witches!" Thunder Throat threw up his hands and walked out.

Two days later, Thunder Throat had fifty warriors gathered in the plaza. He laid out a plan to systematically scour the forest east of what used to be Long Pine Village for any sign of activity. "Leave no stone unturned. If you find them, capture at least one and bring her back to me, unharmed. Is that clear? You leave at first light."

The moon of falling leaves would soon end, and cold weather with snow was at hand. When the ten canoes landed at the old village landing, wet snow coated the bare ground and filtered through the trees back away from the river. By the time their camp was set up in the old plaza, the snow was a knuckle deep and still falling. The following morning, after a quick breakfast, they set out in search of anything they could find. After five days, they had found nothing. The hand of snow that had fallen the first day was beginning to melt, making the hillside trails treacherous. After five more days, all the trails were muddy, slippery, and tracked up so badly, it was impossible to read any sign. They returned to Black Bear Village in shame. Two men had injured legs from slipping on the muddy trails and wrenching their knees.

————

UPON THEIR RETURN HOME, Cass and Pena reported success and could not wait to inflict more damage on Thunder Throat's warriors. Tallow convinced them to be patient. He predicted Thunder Throat would do exactly what he did. They stayed away from Long Pine Village grounds until midwinter. The snow was gone but it was cold. Ice lined the banks of the river in the backwaters. The tracked and smeared trails were frozen solid, but they could see how the Black Bear warriors had scoured the area looking for them. A triumphant smile crossed their faces as they shared knowing glances. The next day would mark the start of Pena's moon. She wondered if Red Hand would show up. And would he be alone?

————————

"I WONDERED if you would be here after these past two moons," Pena said to him.

"The superstitious warriors believe the witch story, while others are still skeptical. Thunder Throat is still convinced it was you two stirring up trouble. He is very moody. I think he could be lured into action with another witch sighting," Red Hand told Pena.

"Then we need to get some more hunters out here. Can you do that?" she asked.

"I think I could get Buckthorn and maybe High Hawk to go on a hunt. Drum Wing is afraid of his own shadow, and Fast Feet stays with Thunder Throat. He is becoming more trusted than me," Red Hand stated. "Give me ten days. Hopefully, we will have a good tracking snow by then."

"We will take out one of them and make sure the other sees a witch," Pena said, her mind racing ahead, "but you will see nothing."

————————

BUCKTHORN FOLLOWED the deer tracks in the finger deep fresh snow. Red Hand volunteered to loop around to the northwest and suggested High Hawk go southwest. Surely the deer would not escape them. As High Hawk passed by a small, dense spruce tree with his eyes trained where he thought the deer might be, he caught a slight movement near the ground by his left side. A fraction of a heartbeat later his knee buckled, and he was teetering toward the ground, his knee a ball of fire. He had never felt such searing pain. Tears welled in his eyes as he saw the figure in the crow feather cape and red face standing over him.

"Warrior, I thought I made it clear that Black Bear warriors were not to be hunting in my forest. Buckthorn will be here after hearing you cry out like that. Get him to take you back with a message that says, 'Stay out of my forest!'" She turned and was gone. He lay there writhing in pain and thinking about Skullbreaker and Three Shots who were now worthless beggars because they could no longer hunt. He would soon join them. Skullbreaker would not live the winter because he was too weakened to even beg. The scratchy female voice haunted his thoughts.

Soon High Hawk heard brush moving and knew someone was coming to his aid. Buckthorn appeared, his face pale and shaken. His left arm dangled helplessly at his side, obviously broken. The sweat on his face told High Hawk his friend was in severe pain. "She just appeared on the trail. Without saying a word, the witch smashed my upper arm with her club. She turned and was gone. She never said anything," Buckthorn sounded as if he were in shock.

He will not be able to help, thought High Hawk. He started yelling for Red Hand.

In about a hand of time, Red Hand showed up and helped High Hawk to his good leg, laid his arm over his shoulder and started for the canoe landing. Buckthorn followed without talking, his eyes darting in all directions.

———————

Thunder Throat bellowed, "That is enough!" Everyone was sure he could be heard throughout the valley.

"Tomorrow, we leave to hunt that scum! They will not get away from me! We will chase them all the way to Monongahela Village if need be. It is about time Corn Stalk paid for harboring our enemies!" Thunder Throat yelled to the nearly ten-tens of warriors he had gathered in the plaza as a fresh snow swirled out of a gray sky.

Overnight the storm unleashed its fury. By

morning, snow was more than knee deep inside the stockade and still falling with no sign of surcease. Travel was impossible. For three days, snow fell, the wind blew, and temperatures dropped. When the snow finally abated and the wind died, the temperature plummeted further. The river froze over and drifted deep with snow. There would be no war walk for many days. The second half of the winter stayed cold and snowy like no one could remember. The Hunger Moon was truly a Starving Moon. The equinox came and went without notice. Thunder Throat's fury simmered unabated.

CHAPTER 21
SCOUTING

A typical day for Cass and Pena, when they were not out hunting, was long and arduous. They would wake shortly before the sky began to gray with the new dawn, dress in dirty 'hermit' clothes, sip a cup of leftover tea, and chew on a piece of dried meat.

Their clothing consisted of a dark-tanned buckskin shirt with fringe on the sleeves and no decoration of any kind. A plain brown doeskin breechclout was tied with a rawhide thong around their waists. Dark buckskin leggings covered their legs and high, plain moccasins covered their feet up to the knee. Their shirts came down to about mid-thigh. A sash of coarse woven hemp fiber tied at the left hip for a belt that hugged their slim waists.

From those belts hung pouches for fire making, emergency sewing (for clothing or skin), clay pipes, and smoking material. Each had a sharp bone stiletto slipped into the weave of their belt for quick access if needed. Hanging from their belts was also a chert knife hafted to a deer antler handle. Both young women had a war club hanging on their right hip. The one Cass carried was the Caddoan war club the trader, Traveler, had given her in exchange for her lighter woman's club. Hardly a fair trade. Cass's new club was worth ten times what her old one was. Pena's was heavier than what a typical woman would carry, but nothing like the one Cass carried.

After swallowing their tea and jerky, they each grabbed their bows, quivers, and pouches containing a cloth for cleaning wounds, a small assortment of dried and ground healing plants, and some extra food. Attached to the bag was a rolled elk hide sleeping blanket. They never knew if they would be gone for a half a day, overnight, or several days.

From their small lodge, they would move as fast as they could to one of several trails that led to the canoe landing outside Monongahela Village. Each day they would take a different trail to hide their travel habits. Once on a given trail, they would run as fast as possible to their canoe at the landing. The goal Cass set was to get there in a shorter period each time they went.

Once there, they would board their canoe and paddle up the Spirit Water River to a certain landmark. Again, the goal was to make it to that landmark faster each time. These forays were designed to make them stronger and give them more stamina. They would need both strength and stamina.

They carried out this routine each day, in every kind of weather, from the beginning of their ten-and-fifth summer. Now, at ten-and-seven summers, they felt they could run longer and harder than anyone.

Each day, when they returned to their lodge, they engaged in combat training with Tallow. Using cottonwood war club replicas, they learned the maneuvers needed to fight in a serious situation. Though Cass had already proved herself by killing one of Thunder Throat's warriors with her war club one sun cycle past, she worked and trained harder than ever.

When the snow and cold made river travel too dangerous, Cass and Pena fashioned snowshoes of willow hoops and rawhide mesh and trekked for hands of time through the forests and meadows south of their lodge. The purpose being to strengthen their leg muscles and build stamina.

As suggested by Traveler, Cass practiced catching small mammals, birds, and reptiles with her bare hands. By the end of her ten-and-sixth summer, she could snatch a rattlesnake behind its head in mid-strike to avoid being bitten. Everything she worked at, she was successful at, increasing her confidence with each accomplishment.

———

FIVE DAYS FOLLOWING THE EQUINOX, the harsh winter lost its grip on the land. The skies cleared and temperatures rose quickly. Snow in the higher country melted and the river became clogged with ice first, then uprooted trees brought down through the valleys with the flood waters.

Unable to contain himself any longer, Thunder Throat ordered a forced march over land to the forest around the old Long Pine Village site to find and capture the *witches* that haunted his dreams during his restless nights. It would take eight days slogging through swamps and sloughs in the valleys and muddy hillsides on the slopes. But if he had to, Thunder Throat would lead his army all the way to Monongahela Village to find those women who were harassing his men.

EXPECTING RETALIATION FOR THEIR *WITCHING*, Cass and Pena enlisted an old friend, Tall Man, to help them. There was a series of ridges that pushed from the high country out to the Spirit Water River about halfway between the old site of Long Pine Village and Black Bear Village. In the series, one was known to the Monongahela People as High Ridge. From it a person could see over two ridges to the north and east. The next one, a bit lower, they called Rock Ridge because the ridgeline featured many large, broken boulders that made ideal hiding places among the trees. The third one they called Bald Ridge. It was lower still, and the trees grew sparsely due to very thin soil. From Rock Ridge or High Ridge, a person could see anyone crossing Bald Ridge. Cass and Pena knew that Thunder Throat's scouts would be the first, and hardest to see among the sparse trees on Bald Ridge.

Cass, Pena, and Tall Man left Monongahela Village as soon as the weather began to improve. They were prepared for a long wait. That meant slogging along on wet, melting, drifted snow for days on snowshoes. The Monongahela and lower ends of the Spirit Water were not ice clogged, so they made a couple of days' travel by canoe. But they had to give that up when the river began to rise. They made the hill ground and watched the ice-clogged river overflow its banks. They tied the canoes to trees on land high enough to avoid the flood waters.

When Cass and her two companions reached High Ridge, the snow had melted off the highest areas of the ridges. The weather was clear with warm days and frosty nights. Thunder Throat's warriors could move fast enough over the ridges, but the valleys were a mess with muddy trails, melting snow, and flooding creeks. Cass was happy to note that no one had been there since the previous autumn.

From an ancient spreading chestnut tree near the crest of High Ridge they could view the other ridges well enough to see if anyone was present. By observing, they agreed it would take two hands of time to get from the top of High Ridge to the top of Rock Ridge and a bit more from Bald Ridge to the top of Rock Ridge. As soon as they would see scouts working their way across Bald Ridge, Cass and Pena would start for Rock Ridge. They would be in a position to intercept the scouts before they reached the top of Rock Ridge. Tall Man would hurry back to Monongahela Village to warn Corn Stalk to get her defenses ready—Thunder Throat would be coming if Cass and Pena did not stop him.

The girls had known Tall Man all their lives and thought of him by his childhood name, Green Leaf. He had been the one who could always run farther than anyone else, winning the distance run at every Solstice Celebration. As he became a man, he grew long and lanky legs and still did not tire while running. No one could get from High Ridge to Monongahela Village faster than Tall Man.

Just when gray light streaked across the sky, a lone wolf howl echoed through the river valley. Cass knew she was not alone on that first morning of their watch. The ensuing days gave Cass time to prepare herself for her encounter with Thunder Throat.

As the sun broke over the eastern hills on the fifth day after they reached the top of High Ridge, Tall Man called from the chestnut, "They are coming!" He scrambled down from the tree, gathered his things, and set out for Monongahela Village. Most of the snow was gone now, but the mud and the high water remained in the valleys. The young women reviewed the plan, said their farewells quickly, and he was on his way.

Cass and Pena looked at each other and said, "This is it!" and started down the steep slope. They arrived at Rock Ridge and went to a vantage point where they could see the valley between them and Bald Ridge. Pena spotted a person fighting his way across the small, flooded creek at the bottom. The water was obviously deeper than the warrior was tall, and it was moving swiftly.

"Good, it will take them longer," they said in unison.

But soon enough, all five Black Bear scouts had crossed and were starting up the slope toward them. It was still early morning. The scouts did not dare stop and dry their wet buckskins for fear that Thunder Throat would punish them for the delay. Cass moved to the northwestern most trail, while Pena went to the most southeastern one. They were about three-tens-of-tens of paces apart.

When the Black Bear scouts were close enough, they could see that the farthest northwest was Drum Wing—he should die because of his unfaltering loyalty to Thunder Throat. Next was Fisher—he should die also. Next was Red Hand—of course, he would live. Next, was Two Hearts—he would be captured to serve as a witness. Last was Fast Feet—he and Red Hand would survive and run back to Thunder Throat. Fast Feet would see a witch in a black cape with a red face.

The plan worked perfectly. Drum Wing made it to the top of the ridge first. By the time he worked his way up the muddy trail, his body had warmed, and his leather clothing was nearly dry. When he stopped, steam rose from the damp buckskins he was wearing. His breath came in loud gasps from exertion on the steep, slick trail. He never saw the arrow that pierced his throat. Next, Fisher, trying to control his heavy breathing so he could hear the sounds around him, thought he heard a noise toward where Drum Wing was supposed to be. He stumbled and died as his world went black when a war club smashed mercilessly against the back of his skull, crushing it.

Fast Feet watched a black figure with a red face step from behind a rock and strike Two Hearts in the back of the head with a war club. He was less than five-tens of paces away. It happened too quickly for him to draw his arrow back and shoot. The figure in black just disappeared into the brush. He wheeled and started back along the hill to get a better look. Suddenly a black and red shaft, tipped by an obsidian point, grazed his right upper arm, and lodged in his damp buckskin shirt. Thinking he was in the presence of a witch, he turned and ran back down the muddy slope, never looking back. When he neared the bottom, Red Hand yelled to him to wait for him. When they met, Fast Feet saw that Red Hand had an arrow that just missed his side and stuck into his shoulder pack.

The arrow looked just like the one sticking through the arm of his own shirt.

"We were the lucky ones!" Red Hand exclaimed as the two came together at the base of the ridge.

Fast Feet held up his arm, grimaced, and said, "Speak for yourself. This hurts like ten-tens of bee stings. Thunder Throat needs to be warned. I do not know if I can make it across the creek. You will need to do it."

"I will not leave you out here with a witch! It looks like it is only a scratch. I will help you get there. It is too dangerous to start a signal fire." Red Hand pushed Fast Feet along the trail. Red Hand could see that Fast Feet's arm was bleeding, but it could not be much because the arrow was hanging loosely in the arm of his shirt. When they were across the creek, a wolf howled from somewhere on Rock Ridge.

CHAPTER 22
CONFRONTATION

Two hands of time before the sun reached its high point in the sky, Red Hand and Fast Feet stumbled upon a lookout on Bald Ridge. "What are you doing back here? You were supposed to signal with smoke if you saw anything," Blue Hawk snarled at Red Hand.

"I must see Thunder Throat immediately. And Fast Feet here is wounded. He needs help!" Red Hand breathlessly yelled.

"Thunder Throat is just over the hill with Falcon. The men are awaiting orders to attack," Blue Hawk answered. "You were supposed to start a signal fire in case you encountered them. We are losing time!" He ran over the hill. Red Hand helped Fast Feet to the camp where he could get aid.

Up the hill came Thunder Throat and Falcon. "Red Hand, what happened? Why no fire?"

"She picked us off one by one, Great War Chief. I was lucky, if it were not for my bag, this would be in my back!" He held up his bag with the black and red arrow sticking out.

"How could she do that? You *were* spread out, were you not?"

"Yes, Great War Chief. I do not know how she did it. I know I only saw one figure dressed in a black cape with a bright red face. I was still at the base of the ridge when, to my right, I saw Drum Wing fall to the ground at the top of the hill. I never saw Fisher. As you ordered, I started up the hill in the center to try to see what was happening when I saw Fast Feet scrambling down the hill. I ran to see what he had seen. That is when this arrow hit me. I stumbled at the impact, got up, and kept running to him. When I got to him, I saw he had been wounded in the arm. I looked back and saw the black cape with a red head. It was holding a bow with a nocked arrow. I am starting to believe in witches." Red Hand hung his head in shame.

"Everyone seems to believe in witches around here. Come on, Falcon, let us go *witch* hunting! Red Hand, watch for my signal. Bring the warriors when you see a column of white smoke. When you get to that ridge, we will have a *witch*, maybe two, on a pole. Then we will go to Monongahela Village and teach Corn Stalk the folly of playing *witch* games with Thunder Throat." Thunder Throat winked at Red Hand and smiled at Falcon. The two seasoned war leaders started down the trail.

"We stay together until we get to the base of Rock Ridge where they cannot see us. You will move along the base until you get to the southeast trail. I will proceed up this northwest one in three fingers of time. Do not confront anyone. Wait until we have the pinchers set. The signal is a fox bark. Then we will spring in and teach this girl—or these girls a lesson they will not forget until they die—very, very slowly," Thunder Throat whispered, a demonic grin on his painted face.

Once Falcon separated from Thunder Throat, he began to get a different idea. *He is sending me down the base of the ridge because he wants her first. I think it is time I came first. I will show him. I can move like a ghost, too. I will get up there and have her legs parted before he gets to the top.* Falcon got to his position and scrambled up the hill as quickly and quietly as he could. He was feeling confident because the spring birds were making their courting sounds as if it were a typical spring day. A wood thrush was making its flute-like sound somewhere not far away. He cleared the top and made his way to the middle of the ridge. The wood thrush stopped singing, but Falcon did not notice.

Falcon neared one of the big blocks of stone laying on the surface. Suddenly, out stepped a figure dressed in a crow feather cape and a cardinal feather mask. The figure held a bow drawn with an obsidian tipped arrow pointed at his chest.

"Greetings, Second War Chief," a calm and confident female voice said. "Drop your bow," she continued, with no urgency in her voice.

He assessed the situation and concluded, *I can duck under her aiming point and be on her legs before she blinks an eye.* He dropped like a fallen rock, but when he went to move, something was wrong. His breath was caught, he was hot, he could not move. *It is...getting...dark,* was his final thought. Her arrow pierced his throat, slicing through his voice box, his esophagus, and nicked a jugular vein before shattering a vertebra and separating his spinal cord. The broken obsidian point protruded out the back of his neck. He was dead before his face landed on the ground.

That answers that question. I can kill a man when need be. I already know Cass can. A red-shouldered hawk scolding, "Skriieeeee!" announced to Cass that one less predator walked on the ridge.

CASS WAITED TENSELY on the northeastern trail. She had hidden the witch costume and wore a dull gray-brown hunting shirt sans decoration. Her leggings matched. She had taken a burned stick end and drawn irregular vertical lines of charcoal on her shirt and leggings. At random intervals, she made little horizontal lines. Her head was shaved. With bear grease mixed with ash, she painted her hands, face, and head a dull gray/brown color. The overall result was that when she stood still next to the ancient chinquapin in front of her, it was difficult to know she was there. She even colored the limbs of her bow to match the tree's bark. Now she nervously awaited the arrival of her adversary.

———

THUNDER THROAT WORKED his way around to the river side of the ridge so that he would come up in a place where whoever was waiting up there would not expect. He negotiated the trail as silent as a mountain lion stalking a deer. He listened to every sound, concentrated on every smell. A tufted titmouse called from the top of a tree near the trail halfway up the hill.

As he neared the top, his nostrils picked up a faint but unmistakable whiff of human feces. That confused him. *She surely would not relieve herself if she were hiding.* When he topped the steep hillside, the odor clarified. It was the scent of a human's violent death. The bowels and bladder relaxed and released their refuse as the victim expired. In this case, it was one of his warriors. *Fool!* he thought.

He moved silently forward. Suddenly there was the "Skriieeeee!" of a red-shouldered hawk off to the southeast. He looked in that direction, searching for movement. He did not see the hawk, but he spotted a black figure with a red head gliding between two small trees many paces to the southeast on this very trail. *Witch...pfft! Just a girl in a costume. Why has Falcon not barked?* Hugging the ground, he slowly nocked an arrow in his powerful war bow. He crept silently along the trail to close the gap between himself and his target. The intense scent of death told him he must be close to his dead warrior. Slowly he moved past an old chinquapin. The odor got stronger. He kept moving, one fraction of a step at a time.

———————

CASS WAITED QUIETLY by her tree. She had brushed every twig and leaf from the base of the tree so she could move around it silently, if need be. She listened to every sound the forest made. She noted especially that the tufted titmouse that had been calling his *"peter-peter-peter"* on the river end of the ridge had fallen silent. The small bird moved to another location down the hill and took up his hopeful song. Cass moved to the opposite side of the tree, knowing which trail her enemy was taking. Pena's red-shouldered hawk call got her attention, too. It told her that Falcon was dead.

She noted the hulk of a man who was silently creeping a few paces away, passing her tree just as Pena let out her call.

Cass felt the memories crashing down on her like a great waterfall. It took every ounce of willpower and strength she had to stifle a gasp as her eyes took in the monstrous warrior. She closed her eyes to still the tears that formed there. The images of him on her mother, then brutally mutilating the woman came to her in vivid color. There was no reason, no purpose to do what he did. She tried to steel herself for the task ahead, confidence completely drained.

Am I really going to fight that monster? She questioned her own sanity. *My souls are loose. Better to put an arrow in his back and be done with it. No, that would betray Wolf. Thunder Throat must know that it was the daughter of Yellow Lotus that killed him. Please be with me, Wolf. Whether I live or die is in your hands. The time for thinking is over.* She carefully nocked one of the arrows she had leaned lightly against the tree. The second she held in her left hand so she could reload her bow in less than a heartbeat. She stepped out into the trail less than ten paces behind the big man.

———

THUNDER THROAT HELD his nocked arrow in place with a finger on his left hand and his right fingertips gently holding the bowstring and the arrow at the nocking point. He could draw back and fire accurately in less than a heartbeat. He had practiced it until it was just another motion as natural as breathing. The speed of his bow had cost many enemies their lives. He was quite comfortable that he could not be surprised.

Cass noted Thunder Throat's beautiful bow. It was highly polished choke cherry, laminated with softened bone and sinew for added strength. He was probably the only man strong enough to draw it. *What a shame that I must destroy such a beautiful weapon.*

Thunder Throat saw a flicker of black crossing the trail and moving into a cluster of white cedar trees about six-tens of paces in front of him. He raised the bow, searching for a positive target. Suddenly a blur passed his left side, and his bow lurched out of his hands. *Thwack!* the noise came to his ears. He watched his bow flutter in the air in front of him, even as a stinging sensation burst through the hand that no longer gripped his bow. The black and red arrow struck just above his hand. A loud *Crack!* and the upper limb of his bow folded back, broken by the arrow penetrating it and the strain of the tight sinew bowstring. As he wheeled around, he looked for a target for the throwing knife that was coming out of his waist belt.

"Greetings, Great War Chief," a calm, confident female voice said to him. "Now, now. I would drop that knife if I were you. You would not want to end up like Drum Wing over here, or Fisher down the ridge. You drop the knife and move over to that small clearing," she indicated the area with no trees a few paces away, "and I will lower my bow."

At first glance, all he saw was a big chinquapin. When the person standing in front of it came into focus, it was too late. She had him pinned with a drawn arrow at less than ten paces. He was confused. He had never seen an adversary like this one. It was obviously a young woman. Her plain hunting shirt belted at the waist fit tight enough to indicate her shapely body. With her arms and legs covered, it was difficult to read her muscle tone. But he was intrigued, nonetheless. He felt the surge of blood into his loins as he studied her feminine assets. *Which one is it?* he asked himself, wondering why the arrow struck his bow, and not his back. *Did her fright affect her aim?*

He looked curiously at her. "You and your sister pretending to be witches now-a-days, are you? You are a curious looking one. Two spirit?"

"Don't think I won't shoot. I have killed some of your men today because they would not listen, including your Second, Falcon. Now drop the knife!" she said coldly and looked straight into his eyes, something the trader, Traveler, had told her. "*A man's eyes will betray his motions. Before he can take an action, he must calculate the consequences. That requires looking, shifting eyes, glancing...sometimes almost imperceptible, but always.*" Thunder Throat's eyes looked back at her and saw the intent.

He dropped the knife, turned, and started for the clearing. "You can ambush me now, shoot me in the back. That is what you do, is it not?" he chided her. He noted she did not tell him to drop his war club. *What a fool!* He confidently walked out into the clearing, turned, and held his big hands out to his sides, palms up.

———

I AM A FOOL. Cass glanced at his massive war club. It looked to be made of ash with a smooth curve from the handle up to the curled end that held a large, round granite rock. Protruding from the end where the wood ended was a short, square copper peg formed into a sharp point. It stuck out half a finger in length. On the round impact surface of the rock was another round, blunt copper plug. It would punch a knuckle-width hole in any bone it contacted. Overall, it was half again bigger than any club she had ever seen. His huge muscular arms promised he could swing the big club as hard and often as he wanted to.

The midafternoon sun shone through the deciduous trees covered with bulging buds, giving the ground a dappled look and warmed the air in the clearing. *It all comes down to this moment. Nine sun cycles since that night. Wolf, I hope you are still with me,* she repeated her earlier prayer. With him ten paces away, she lowered her bow and set it carefully against a tree. "So, you know who I am?"

"Yes, I know you are one of Yellow Lotus's twins. But it matters little to me which one. I must say, I do look forward to driving my big manhood into your panic-dried woman hole and tearing your delicate tissue apart. You owe me for the good bow you destroyed. Before this afternoon passes, you will wish you had put that arrow in my back. I hope you fight harder than your mother did. I will use you until I tire of it, maybe a few of my men will as well. Then I think I will tie you to a stake in the Black Bear Village Plaza. The wives of the warriors you have crippled will be happy to watch you die one small piece at a time. Just before you pass, I think I will cut your heart out and eat it. You owe me for making me wait all these sun cycles," he said mockingly.

"Great War Chief, as inviting as your plan sounds, I have a different idea. It involves you laying on the ground writhing in pain and realizing you will never hurt another human being," she answered confidently.

"Your confidence is unbecoming for a woman. Your mother was also confident—until I destroyed her. My manhood was too much for her, you know. Too bad you could not have seen her pathetic *fight.*" He laughed sarcastically.

"I was there. I witnessed the whole thing. What you did to her unborn child was less than human. Horned Serpent would not even think of doing that," she came back, challenge in her voice. She noted his eyes open wider at that revelation. "Our aunt hid us in the secret tunnel. We were right there under the rocks in the plaza. We saw and heard everything."

"So, what do you intend to do about it? Are you

going to fight me with that little war club? Ha-ha. Do you have any idea how many men I have killed?" he challenged. He noted her war club was different than any he had ever seen. It was straight-handled and had a narrow, oval-shaped white rock about the size of his big fist. The rock was held in place by rawhide wrapped over the end in a groove ground into the stone then set into a notch cut in the handle and twisted several times around the handle. The shaft was a type of wood he did not recognize. It was coarse-grained, a dark orange with the grain dark brown in color. It looked very stout and was by no means a woman's club. *She is delusional if she thinks she can fight against me with that, or any other club. She is just a girl. She must live in a dream world.*

"Great War Chief, you need to take credit for the women and babies, too. And how many little boys have there been? Give me the complete total," she returned his challenge.

"Your insolence and misplaced confidence will be your undoing," he proudly announced. Chuckling, he leaned his club against a tree at the edge of the clearing.

"And your arrogance will be yours." She took the war club from her belt and stepped into the clearing.

CHAPTER 23
THE FIGHT

C ass stood in a ready position, knees bent slightly, feet just past shoulder-width apart primed to move in any direction. Her empty left hand was out to her side and a little forward for balance. She held her club in her right hand just above waist-high and level. She was ready to react to any action he took.

Nine sun cycles were not enough, nine more would not be enough, but it is too late for running away. Cass felt her heart pounding faster against her ribs. The blood pounding in her ears sounded like a grouse drumming. Spring bird songs took on the sound of demons screeching. Leaves rattling on the forest floor sounded like a tornado was bearing down on her. *I am like a forest mouse facing a great bear. I pray he cannot see my trem-*

bling knees and sense my fear. Right now, I am as good as dead. Still, if the mouse can avoid the claws and jaws, and manage to bite the bear in the right places...

A familiar voice echoed in Cass's mind. *You will fail if you dwell on your fear. Follow your instincts.*

Cass took a deep breath. Her pounding heart slowed. The cacophony of spring bird songs fell silent, and the rustle of the wind through the dry leaves on the forest floor hushed. The world went into slow motion around her as Cass looked across the clearing. Meeting the direct stare of the huge man standing only ten paces away, every muscle in her body tingled. The sky brightened, and her vision became more acute. She could see each wrinkle around his eyes despite the black war paint.

Cass looked deeply into his eyes. She looked into his souls, only to sense a void. *He has no life-soul. I should have known. He is a predator, and his goal was always to cause pain and suffering.*

Nine sun cycles of preparation brought Cass to this moment. Every bone, every muscle, every sinew, every nerve had been honed to confront this man. Now, as her world focused through her eyes, she could almost read his mind. As her adversary scrutinized her from head to toe, she could see his plan forming before he did.

I am ready, she admonished herself and refocused.

In a blur, Thunder Throat charged in low, trying to grab one of her legs. The attack was ineffective as she easily sidestepped his charge. The young woman took a deep breath and turned to face him again. She noted how he glanced from her club to her feet, then to her free hand.

Just breathe. 'Follow your instincts,' as Wolf told you, she reminded herself.

In a lightning-quick move, her nemesis went toward her free hand, as she expected. Again, she lightly stepped away from his lunge, and slapped his lower back with her hand as he drove past her. Growling, he wheeled and grasped for her, but only caught air. The once arrogant smile no longer resided on his black-painted face.

The massive man made another charge for her. This time, he feinted to her right before going after her left leg. Anticipating the attack, Cass jumped back. Once again, Thunder Throat only came up with air.

The young woman could see the frustration building in the warrior's eyes. His chest rose and fell with increased anger. Snorting like an enraged bull elk, he leaped for her again, but she ducked out of the way, causing him to roar. Incensed, his eyes rolled in their sockets.

Thunder Throat stepped back, assessing the situation as he sucked in a heavy breath and worked to calm his agitated nerves. Seeing the red of chaos, he gathered his wits, saw an opening, and charged. Missing his target, he twirled around and dove at her again and again.

Her narrow escapes caused the drums in her ears to pound louder. *That was too close!* Her eyes widened as he stood up, preparing for another attack. She noted that sweat poured from his forehead, and how his bare chest glistened. She was sweating, too, but not like him. *If I can keep moving, maybe I can wear him down. That may give me an opening.*

When Thunder Throat picked up his huge war club and stalked toward her, she recognized his shift in attitude. The game became ominously more dangerous. She knew he was one with that weapon. He had breathed his predator soul into it, he cherished it, and it gave him much more reach —and confidence. It had just become more difficult to evade his attacks.

The warrior assaulted her, swinging the big mace through the air in a figure-eight pattern that swooshed and whistled frighteningly close to her face. Desperately trying to remain in control, Cass feinted one way, and then the other. She struggled to keep in rhythm with his movements, dancing around the small clearing.

She is like a spirit. She moves one way and then is not there. I have never faced an enemy so quick on their feet! But she will tire, Thunder Throat thought, as he tried to slow his breathing.

He lunged where he expected his target to retreat with no reward. Though she barely avoided his heavy club, the young woman always made the right decision, thwarting his attempts to maim her.

Spirit helpers are guiding her movements, he thought apprehensively. *It is as if she can read my mind. Perhaps there is some truth to the witch stories.*

He is getting tired, but I am also growing weak. My legs ache, and tremble when I stand still. I cannot let him see my weariness, she told herself. She shifted her sweat-soaked hunting shirt to gain better freedom of movement.

Thunder Throat's chest was heaving as he tried to catch his breath. His efforts seemed to be increasingly laborious after each attack, which encouraged the young woman. Still, she knew the seasoned warrior was far from finished, and her chances for success remained slim.

If I do not falter, I will have an opportunity soon. I must be ready! She steeled herself for the next onslaught.

Thunder Throat leveled his swing at Cass's shoulder. When she ducked low, he shifted his angle downward. She noted that when the big club hit the ground, it stayed there for the briefest bit of a heartbeat, the heavy ball sunk partially into the soil. It also occurred to her that when he started swinging that heavy club toward the ground, even *he* had to let it land, no longer able to stop it in mid-swing.

When Thunder Throat unleashed his next attack, Cass ducked down again. He followed her movement, slashing the big mace downward once more.

Until that moment, she had only employed her club to help her maintain balance, never able to make an offensive move. Still, her shoulder and arm were growing stiff.

When his club angled downward, she jumped back. This time, as his club whistled past her arched-back chest toward the ground, Cass whipped her club around, switched to her left hand, and the instant his club contacted the ground, she drove hers into the back of his big hand. The rounded hard white rock slammed into the back of his hand with a loud, meaty *splat*! A sickening *crunch* resounded as the small bones in the warrior's massive hand shattered.

"Ayieeeeeeee!" he roared as he drew back his

wounded hand. The pain instantly made him nauseous. With his left hand, he held his throbbing right hand up and looked at it. It was already changing colors from its normal light brown to red and purple. The palm was swollen and misshapen, with three fingers straight and pointing off in obtuse directions. His thumb and smallest finger were clenched so tightly the pain was nearly unbearable. He turned a murderous gaze toward her and started for her.

Quickly, he realized his only weapon lay on the ground. As he went in to pick it up in his left hand, he noticed her approaching, preparing another blow with her menacing club. He frantically kicked at her with his right leg as she drew close. His foot glanced off her shoulder, but it was enough to send her sprawling, dropping her club. Her thwarted attack gave him enough time to grip his club in his left hand and wildly swing it in her direction.

She managed to roll away from him and came to her feet out of his range. But now she was empty-handed, and he stood, shoulders hunched, sucking in air, between her and her club where it lay on the ground. He took a couple of steps back, his throbbing right hand pinned against his chest. When he looked down at her club, a confident smile grew on his sweaty face, and he drew his club back. When Thunder Throat's club struck the handle of her club, it would shatter, rendering the weapon useless.

Cass timed her leap perfectly, slamming her right foot into the broken right hand against his muscular chest as his big club swung down toward her prized possession. His body twisted from the force of the impact. His left arm, carried by the momentum of the swinging club, missed its intended target, arching his arm back and straining his shoulder. As he floundered for balance, she landed on her left foot, ducked, rolled, and came back to her feet with her club in hand.

He came at her like a madman, swinging his club wildly, again using a figure-eight pattern to change the momentum of his swing from left to right. Now she found it easier to avoid contact with his wildly flashing weapon. The warrior's big arm tired, and his frustration grew. His swings became more predictable. His obvious pain and lack of success was lifting her spirits, giving her a surge of energy.

At last, Cass timed one of his passes, and when his arm was extended, slashing in front of her, she countered with a powerful swing using both hands into the outside of his elbow. Again, a horrific splat of the hard stone on skin accompanied breaking bone. His entire left forearm went limp instantly, the club falling harmlessly to the ground. His elbow, at the impact point, hurt worse than his right hand. He staggered back in searing pain, calling her every unbecoming name he could think of.

Cass circled him, studying his weakened body and hateful glaring eyes. "Why is it that you hate so much, Great War Chief?" she asked him, panting as she talked, genuinely wanting to know. He only hissed at her.

Why do I hate? Thunder Throat was born to hate. I killed my mother while birthing me. The aunt that gave me her tit told me I was more demon than boy. He worked to steady his stance.

Cass observed his face while Thunder Throat blinked, trying to regain his composure. "You can tell me all of it, Great War Chief. You are as good as dead now, and no one will ever know what drives you unless you tell me," she said in a sympathetic tone.

"Look for no pleas of mercy from me, witch. I am wounded, but not dead," he growled through gritted teeth.

She is no different than the others. As I began to grow bigger than the other children, they mocked me, said I killed my own mother. When I talked differently than everyone, they mocked me more. I would not put up with that, so I hurt them. It was my pleasure to hurt them. *I laughed when they cried, just like the aunt who had made me cry. They learned to fear and respect me. But she was the first person to die at my hand. No one ever figured out who killed her or why.*

"Great War Chief, you have said I am only playing a witch to frighten your men. I will tell you that you are right. It has been a great game to get you out here to face me alone." The sympathy was gone from her voice.

Playing games, just like my father. My father... what a weakling—a fool. I hated his 'peace' game. I still do. I hated him for it. I prided myself in putting Black Wolf's arrow through his heart. It made me strong, and the warriors recognized my strength, following me without question. They became my warriors.

Now I stand before this witch who has broken me. She has no idea how much that increases my hate!

He charged at her trying to kick her. *Anywhere, just make contact, hurt her,* he willed himself. She avoided every kick. His broken hand and arm were slowing him down dramatically, and he knew it. *She is waiting for a chance to kill me. It will not come easy. Where are my warriors? Have they abandoned me? I must attack to keep her on the defensive until Red Hand arrives.*

Cass knew she had the advantage now. But she still recognized how dangerous his feet were.

"With your defeat here today, Black Bear Village will once again walk the path of peace. You do know that do you not, Great War Chief? Your people do not like you," she said sympathetically, but with truth on her tongue.

No! My men...they are too many...too strong. I have made them strong. They are loyal to me. Red Hand will be on this ridge any time now, he thought while trying to think of some way to stop this witch from killing him.

"Falcon is dead. Red Hand awaits our signal that you are no more. He will marry my sister, help rebuild Long Pine Village, and you will be but a distant, bad memory," Cass calmly told him while catching her breath.

Then, in a fraction of a heartbeat, she came in low and smashed the outside of his left knee. Again, he cried out in pain as he stood slump-shouldered, trying to maintain balance on his right leg. His eyes were bloodshot and sat in black, hollowed sockets. Sweat poured down his forehead, into his eyes, and dripped off his chin, taking rivulets of his black war paint with it. She twirled and came in hard again, crushing his right kneecap. He fell to the ground helplessly, unable to get out of a painful position. Cass let out a red-shouldered hawk's *"Skriieeeee!"*

Pena answered from just outside the clearing, "I am with you, sister."

Pena pushed Two Hearts into the clearing, his hands bound at the elbows and wrists behind his back. A mink skin ball was in his mouth preventing him from calling out. She withdrew the chert knife she held at his back, sat him down, tied him to a small tree, bound his legs again then, and removed the gag.

"Great War Chief, I am sorry this has happened to you. I was witched and helpless to warn you." Two Hearts was out of breath and nearly crying as he addressed the big man, who suddenly seemed smaller.

Cass reached into a bag she had hidden close by and pulled out several lengths of hemp rope. She tied one around each of Thunder Throat's ankles. He was helpless, unable to stop her. "I would like you to meet my sister, Great War Chief. But you said you care not."

"Finish it, you witch," he growled, barely understandable.

"Now, Great War Chief, would you let one of your enemies off so easily? I think not. And you do not believe in witches, remember? Why do you call me a witch?" Cass asked, now with no sympathy in her voice.

Cass and Pena each took a rope and stretched

his legs wide apart and tied the ropes to trees. The weakness in his broken knees kept him from putting up much resistance. He lay on his back trying to scrunch some of the tension off the ropes. It was useless. The overwhelming pain caused him to close his eyes. Cass took the opportunity to loop a rope over his swollen right hand. As he tried to fight it off, Pena looped a rope over his numb left hand. They pulled on the ropes until they had his arms spread wide. The wounded war chief was completely helpless. Again, they tied the stretched ropes off to trees so that he was unable to move at all.

Cass looked around until she found a flat rock about two hands square and one hand thick. She slid it under his right knee. "So far, all your injuries will heal, and you will be able to function again, Great War Chief. I told you my desire is to see you writhing in pain knowing you can never hurt anyone again. Do you remember that, Great War Chief?"

"Finish it," he said hoarsely, his breath coming in pants.

"Not quite yet, Great War Chief," she mocked. "I wonder if I can wield your mighty war club?" she taunted. She dragged it from where it lay on the ground after she had broken his left elbow. She hefted it over her head with both hands and brought it down with all her strength onto his right knee that was propped up on the flat rock.

The sight and sound made Two Hearts look away.

"This is for our mother, Great War Chief. Do you remember shoving the red-hot brand into her woman hole? Do you suppose that felt better than getting your knees crushed?" She moved the flat rock beneath his left knee, then crushed it with his war club.

Then she repeated the procedure with both elbows. "And that was for our father. You see, if you live, I do not want you to be able to use your arms or legs, Great War Chief," she explained in his ear. She turned to Pena. "Do you think Wolf is satisfied now, sister. I cannot imagine inflicting any more pain on this poor man."

"First, I have a gift for the Great War Chief, sister," Pena answered coldly.

She kneeled and said into Thunder Throat's face, "You like gifts, don't you, Great War Chief? I have an arrow for you."

She moved down to his waist, pulled out her chert knife and cut the thongs holding up his breechclout, then pulled the sweaty garment away. She moved and stood between his spread-eagle legs. First, she used the obsidian point of an arrow to push his massive, but flaccid, manhood over his quivering thigh and out of the way. A pink line appeared where the razor-sharp blade slid across the delicate skin of his penis. Then, she lifted her bow and nocked the arrow. She drew back, carefully aimed, and sent the black and red arrow through his scrotum and his fleshy buttock muscles, pinning him to the ground. He barely had enough strength to whimper. "That was better than you did to my father, Great War Chief. And Father never screamed once. Of course, he was a better man than you," she calmly said.

Pena turned to Two Hearts. "I think I have seen enough torture to last a lifetime. What about you, Two Hearts? Are you ready to see peace return to this valley?"

He just nodded, tears running down his cheeks.

CHAPTER 24
VICTORY

While Cass was crushing Thunder Throat's knees and elbows, Pena had started a signal fire.

Cass and Pena stood in the late afternoon sunlight and watched for movement on Bald Ridge while Pena's fire billowed white smoke. Soon they saw figures moving through the sparse brush along the ridge. Cass went to Thunder Throat and whispered in his ear, "Good news, Great War Chief! Your warriors are crossing Bald Ridge. They will be here in less than three hands of time. They will rescue you and you can seek revenge on us, unless they see that you are helpless now, and the elders can select a war chief who is not filled with hate." Thunder Throat opened his bloodshot eyes and looked at her with hate.

"Finish me," he rasped, barely able to move his jaw. Vomit drizzled from his mouth and pooled next to his head.

"Pena and I must leave you now. Enjoy the rest of your life, however long it is, Great War Chief," Cass said her final words to Thunder Throat. "Let us be on our way, Pena."

Pena gave Two Hearts a long drink from her water skin, and the two sisters disappeared over the ridge to the southwest.

Cass and Pena climbed into the spreading chestnut tree on High Ridge just as the sun disappeared over the hills west of the river. In the fading light, they could see the orange glow of Pena's signal fire. They could barely make out figures moving around near it. Soon a larger fire was made close by where Thunder Throat lay on the ground. From the light of that fire, they could see people around a shape on the ground, presumably Thunder Throat. Gradually more fires were started on Rock Ridge. No torches were working their way down the west side of the ridge following Cass and Pena's tracks. There would be no pursuit.

A single torch moved to the west side of Rock Ridge. The holder of the torch waved it back and forth toward High Ridge. "That is Red Hand," Pena said. "I must return his signal." She climbed down and added some White Cedar bows to the small fire she had built when they arrived. The billowing white smoke told Red Hand she received his signal. The torch on Rock Ridge was relit, and the wave signal repeated. "All is well, they are not coming after us, sister." *I wish I could tell him how much I love him and miss him!*

A wolf howled somewhere along the river while Cass trembled uncontrollably. "It-it is...over. The Great War Chief is no more! Wolf's promise fulfilled," Cass sobbed.

———

BACK ON ROCK RIDGE, Red Hand looked at Thunder Throat's contorted face. Gone was the arrogant monster capable of so much pain and suffering. Instead, here was a man defeated in every way. Physically he was wasted, his arms and legs swollen nearly beyond recognition. So many veins and arteries were destroyed that blood flowed into the wounds but had no way to return. He had choked on his vomit and was no longer conscious. His heartbeat had reduced to an almost imperceptible flutter. Blood oozed from his wounded groin. Despite efforts to revive him, he never regained consciousness. As he expired, Red Hand let out a sigh of relief.

He ran and took a burning branch and waved it

to where he knew Pena waited for his signal on High Ridge. Seeing her return signal, he smiled. He wished he could give her the news in person, and not just about Thunder Throat. He had more important news for her. But he was duty bound to stay with the Black Bear warriors. *I wish I could tell her how much I love her and miss her!*

By morning, the Black Bear warriors were ready to return to their village and choose a new war leader. One not like Thunder Throat. It was decided to dismember Thunder Throat's body and scatter the parts far-and-wide. The head was put in a basket, weighed down with rocks, and thrown into the raging river. His spirit soul would wander the forest forever with no path to the ancestors. He did not deserve a traditional burial.

CHAPTER 25
RETURN

The sisters talked of the future while they made their cross-country trek back toward Monongahela Village. The snow was mostly melted and the ground muddy. Their leggings became heavy with wet mud in no time, but their mood was so light they barely noticed. They ignored the inconvenience, so relieved were they that the war chief who haunted their dreams was gone forever.

"Will you take your old name, sister?" Cass asked Pena as they trudged along on their second day.

"I am not sure. I have gotten used to Pena, but my old name was pretty, a gift from our mother. I think of her in the happy days when I think of my old name," Pena answered slowly.

And Red Hand likes Bright Star much better than Pena.

"Then I think you should go back to it. If it makes you smile, then it is proper," Cass replied sincerely.

"But it was a child's name," Pena answered wistfully.

"That child ceased to exist nine sun cycles past. The mourning period is over. The name suits you. You are a bright star. I think you should take it back, as you should take back all of yourself—your name, your clan duties, your place in the new Long Pine Village," Cass pressed.

"All right, I will talk with Water Mint and Corn Stalk about my name. What about you? What are you going to do?" Pena's mind was racing in many directions.

"Your future I can see, sister. You will one day be Head Matron of New Long Pine Village, and Red Hand will be your husband and father of your children. My own future is a gray cloud. I see nothing. Perhaps I was meant to die with the Black Bear War Chief," Cass answered bleakly.

Pena noted that Cass was quiet for a long time as they made their way along a muddy trail above the floodplain of the Spirit Water River. "Are you well, sister?" Pena asked with concern in her voice.

Cass replied, "Just thinking about the war chief

we killed. Before he charged me that first time, I looked deep into his eyes. The world had become calm and quiet to me, my eyes focused like never before. I was trying to see into his souls, to understand why he hated so much. At first I thought there was no life-soul. I thought that was it. He was detached from life, so he could hurt and kill without feeling. Then he attacked me, and I had no more time to think about what I had seen in his eyes."

"Did you see more? I have never looked into someone's eyes and read their souls...well, except Red Hand. I think I saw love in his eyes." Tears filled Pena's eyes as she was reminded of her lost love.

"I think I did see more. Thinking on it, I saw dark pain in the War Chief's souls. Something buried very deep, maybe from early childhood. I will never have the answer, but I almost feel sorry for him. Something hurt him to his core. His reaction was to take that hurt out on everyone else. He must have lived a sad, lonely life." Cass looked far away as she spoke. *Kind of like us.*

Pena was lost in her own sorrows and remained silent until they stopped to make camp for the night.

By the time the young women reached the lower river valley, the weather had turned unseasonably cold. A northwest wind dominated, and most mornings were met with frost.

It took Cass and Pena eight days to get back to the riverbank across from Monongahela Village. The river was high and still rising from melting snow runoff. They found the canoe they had left tied to a tree high above the floodplain. Once they reached the mouth of the Spirit Water, they were forced to paddle up the Monongahela some distance before they could negotiate the turbulent waters to the south bank and to the Monongahela Village landing.

"We expected to see ten-tens of canoes full of angry warriors coming down the river!" Tall Man yelled from the village canoe landing. When they landed, there was a large crowd gathering. Corn Stalk stood by the palisade opening with a regal smile on her pretty face.

"Greetings, Warriors!" Corn Stalk addressed them with a big smile when they closed the distance from the landing to where she stood next to the palisade opening. She looked oddly at Cass. Although the young woman had cleaned up, her hair still looked recently shaved, and her hunting shirt was ugly. "You must tell me everything over some tea in my longhouse. You will need to recount your story many times, I am afraid."

"Yes, many times," Cass said as she thought of

the monotony of standing and pounding a thick oak pestle into a log mortar of dried corn. Then, she saw Water Mint, Tallow, Fingerling, and Dewdrop coming to greet them. "Waiting for us here, were you?" Cass addressed Water Mint.

"More than that, Cass, we have moved all our possessions and burned our wigwam in the rocks. We live here, for now," Water Mint told Cass.

"I am glad you waited to talk to me about it first. Perhaps you did not expect me back?" Cass replied sarcastically.

"We will talk about it later," Water Mint replied, ending the discussion.

Pena was on her knees hugging Fingerling and Dewdrop. Everyone was all smiles, except several young male warriors. Their expressions displayed their jealousy.

In the longhouse, they settled onto mats, and the two young women took turns relating the story of the end of the Black Bear War Chief. No details were left out, and none were embellished, as most warriors tend to do when recounting a great victory.

"Your story will be told for generations. It seems your vision from Wolf was true after all," Corn Stalk said in awe of the two young women. "I am sorry I ever doubted you."

"It is a story that should not have to be told,"

Cass said, sadness in her voice. She was clearly depressed.

"I need to talk to you while it is quiet, Head Matron," Pena said after an uneasy silence.

The four women moved into Corn Stalk's private chamber to talk while Tallow entertained his children. "I am considering whether I should take my old name back," Pena said pensively. She went on to explain why she wanted it back, leaving everything out about Red Hand.

Cass finished for her. "Bright Star will marry Red Hand of Black Bear Village. They will build a longhouse in New Long Pine Village for Head Matron Water Mint and the Water Plant Clan. I can count three clans among the Long Pine refugees who will help build the new village. A peaceful alliance with Black Bear Village will last for many sun cycles. One day, Bright Star will be Head Matron of New Long Pine Village, and Red Hand will be her War Chief and father of her children."

"You can read the future now? You are a Dreamer?" Corn Stalk asked cautiously, though she felt questioning anything Cass said might be a mistake. Pena's face flushed and she looked at her lap where she held her turtle shell cup of sassafras and mint tea.

"I can see Bright Star's future, little else," Cass said honestly.

"What of you? What about your childhood name? What about your future?" Corn Stalk asked tentatively.

"The child that was Bright Moon died in a tunnel nine sun cycles past. I am Cass. In my vision, my future is a gray cloud of fog. I can see nothing," Cass said matter-of-factly, a touch of sadness in her voice.

"I can think of several young men who would gladly court you. You need not have such a bleak future," Corn Stalk said, attempting to sound supportive.

"Head Matron, I am a killer of men. Any man willing to come into my world is a fool. I need time to sort this all out in my own mind. Please do not push anyone on me. I will only resent it," Cass replied blankly.

"You have had a successful war walk. It is a time of feasting and celebration. Your future will work itself out. I am not sure I like the idea of a Black Bear warrior in the family, but it sounds like you approve of him. That means much," Corn Stalk told Cass.

"Shall we rejoin the others and start the feasting?" Corn Stalk addressed all of them.

While moving to the big room, Pena whispered

to Cass, "I do wish you would stop saying Red Hand will be my husband. It cannot be. My heart cries for him, and you are not helping."

"Just telling what I see, sister. And my visions have not been false yet."

"That one is. Please let it go. I beg you!" Pena pleaded.

"I will say no more."

The feasting and storytelling went well into the night. Many elders, friends, and warriors came calling to hear the things Cass and Pena had to say. All the visitors, young and old, listened and smiled politely. But Cass could read the skepticism and disbelief in their eyes. It would be a long time before she would feel comfortable among these people.

Water Mint sat there absorbing the entire saga over and over, with tears in her eyes. "Can it be? Can Long Pine Village be reborn?" she sobbed. "My dear sister..." Water Mint whispered as she watched a whiff of smoke drifting through one of the smoke holes in the top of the longhouse. She fell silent as her shoulders slumped.

———

A FEW DAYS LATER, Water Mint gathered all the Long Pine refugees together to discuss their future.

Although some had married into clans from Monongahela Village, they all supported rebuilding Long Pine Village.

Black Willow spoke up. "Is it true, this Red Hand is my son? You have known this for two sun cycles and kept me in the dark? How could you be so cruel? Why did you keep the truth from me?" She was on the verge of a complete breakdown. Hard Edge held her tight with a tear trickling down his own cheek.

"Because our plan was not formed. We still had to keep things secret. We have been tortured, keeping it secret from you as well. But if any of our plans had been leaked, we would have failed, and Red Hand would be dead for sure, possibly all of us, as well. Please find it in your heart to see the situation from our perspective. We did what we thought was best for everyone," Cass replied, shouldering the responsibility.

Hard Edge spoke for him and Black Willow, "We can see your reasoning, and you may have saved many lives. When can we expect our son to return to us?"

Bright Star hung her head and cried. "H-he will n-not be returning. His adopted mother, Head Matron of the Heron Clan, forced him to marry a Bear Clan woman, and they have a child by now," she sobbed.

Cass stood before the gathering and said in a way that left no room for discussion, "We will discuss that situation later. The old Long Pine Village is dead. That site now belongs to our ancestors. New Long Pine Village will be built on a hill overlooking the river, a half-day north of the old site, on the east side. Just to the north of that site there are lands suitable for growing the three sisters. The new village, built on a hill, will be easier to defend. Our people should go there and lay out the new village during the warm moons and plan to start building after the harvest and Green Corn Celebration here. A sun cycle from now, the new village will be born."

Cass was able to join the men and a few women in the fields preparing the ground, cutting trees, and burning brush in the Monongahela planting fields. She found it much easier to work alongside men than women. The men joked about her strength and made ribald jokes about how her muscular thighs would crush a man. The moment one would get bold enough to suggest intimacy, she could give them a threatening look, and the man would back off.

The women, however, were all about getting her married to this warrior or that one. They relentlessly admonished her for being too muscular. "Men want a soft woman, not a wooden goddess who is stronger than them." Woman after woman lectured her. The thought of working side by side in the fields with those women made her ill. Cass was not a normal woman, and just could not do normal woman things.

Cass turned to hunting most days to provide meat for Corn Stalk's longhouse and the people involved in laying out the New Long Pine Village. Despite the colder than normal weather, she brought home meat nearly every time she went out.

Cass found herself sitting between Fingerling and Dewdrop at Pena's naming ceremony, and enjoyed playing with the children all evening, while most adults danced and consumed black drink. By playing with the children all evening, Cass did not need to talk with the young men gawking at her the entire time.

BRIGHT STAR WOKE up and heard Cass quietly sobbing. They shared a sleeping platform in Corn Stalk's longhouse. "Cass, it's all right. I am right here. Was it the evil war chief again?" Bright Star spoke softly in Cass's ear. She assumed Cass was haunted by her old nightmares.

"Bright Star, my heart sings for your future.

Many joyous things will come to you. In my dream, I saw you with a baby at your breast and a toddler on your hip. Your strong warrior, Red Hand, stood by your side in New Long Pine Village. It was a Solstice Celebration, I think. Water Mint was there, with Tallow at her side. A child was riding on her hip and three others were in the Games. Corn Stalk stood in the middle of the plaza, and a man I could not see clearly was at her side. Even Red Oak and Tall Man stood with their wives and children. The whole village was happy," Cass sobbed as she related her dream.

"Sister, that sounds like a happy dream. Why do you cry?" Bright Star asked, concern in her voice.

"Everyone was there and happy, but there... was..." Cass sobbed, tears flowing down her cheeks, "no Cass."

Bright Star quickly answered, "But you were there, watching. You will always be with us." She did not know how to handle her sister's new melancholy.

"You do not understand. I was watching, yes but from above." Cass's voice cracked and she cried harder. "It-it-it w-was like...I was with...the Ancestors! Cass was...no more! I thought I was ready to die...but I am not." She embraced Bright Star in a death grip, pressing her head into her sister's shoulder.

As they drank tea and ate gruel and corn cakes that morning, Water Mint pulled Cass aside and asked, "Was the former Black Bear War Chief in your dream last night? I wanted to come, but had Dewdrop sprawled across me and did not want her bothering you."

Cass answered in a monotone, "No, I dreamed of the future. Yours looks bright."

"Then, why the tears?" Water Mint asked.

"I have no future. I just want to go to sleep and not wake up." Cass grabbed her bow, quiver, and hunting bag and stomped out of the longhouse.

"We are terribly worried about Cass," Water Mint said to Corn Stalk. She pointed to Bright Star and Tallow. "I have never known her to be so depressed. All through...everything, she was a rock —never like this. She seems to care about nothing."

Bright Star interjected, "She told me about hunting, but not being able to feel anything when killing an animal. 'What's the point?' she said." She shook her head in dismay. "Cass thinks it is a message from Wolf that she is going to die. I am worried sick. And she keeps insisting I will end up with Red Hand. We all know that is not going to happen." Tears formed in her eyes. "I am the one who lost a man. I should be the one depressed. I am so worried about her I do not have time to think about me." A tear trickled down her cheek.

"We need a celebration," Corn Stalk said. "Hang together and support Cass all you can. The Solstice will be here next moon. Maybe men will come along for both of you. For now, I must make sure those three sisters get stuck in the ground, even though the ground is still too cold." Corn Stalk spoke glibly, but her mind was in turmoil.

CHAPTER 26
RUMORS

"Thank you for coming to my room, Cass. Do you feel like talking?" Corn Stalk asked when she was sure they were alone.

"About what?"

"It will soon be a moon since you returned from your war walk. But you do not seem to be fitting in. The women tell me you are unfriendly, and the men are asking if you are *two spirit* because you reject every warrior who comes to court you. Some are even questioning if maybe you really are a witch. I know better than that, of course. But rumors can be harmful if allowed to continue," Corn Stalk said in her best motherly way.

"Grandmother, the men that are sent to court me are of three kinds. More than half see me as a mankiller and quiver in my presence. They look at me as a rabbit behind a single blade of grass in a bare meadow trying to hide from a fox. Others look at me as if they are the fox, and they think I should fear them. A few look at me as if they are an eagle flying over that helpless rabbit.

"The man I accept to court me will look at me as the eagle looks at his mate. He knows she is deadly but loves her for his whole life. He looks at her as an equal and does so on the day he first lays on her. I will accept nothing less. I have yet to meet a man who will even look me in the eye, let alone see my blackened souls. Do you understand me?"

"Yes. But men cannot see you as an equal if you do not let them get to know you. I feared this when you insisted on living out there in the forest. You have had no chance to have friends and share experiences. What will become of you?

"I need all the women in the fields tomorrow, planting corn. Will you be there?" Corn Stalk asked sharply, changing the subject.

"No. I cannot work side by side with women who scorn and scold me for not being like them. I will hunt and bring back meat to feed your planters. They will not appreciate it, but I care not," Cass answered easily.

"You can work with Water Mint and Bright

Star. I can tell the others to leave you alone," Corn Stalk offered.

"I would rather hunt. I can feel a change in the weather. I think it is going to warm up, finally," Cass replied.

"I feel that as well. The wind is already shifting. I wish we could get you to see the world more like the woman you are, who you were born to be. Please forgive me for asking, but do you feel you have *attractions*, like some who are two spirit?" Corn Stalk asked sadly, and held Cass's hand,

"Grandmother, ask Water Mint and Bright Star —I never saw the world like a normal girl. I always wanted to chase butterflies and hunt rabbits instead of learning to weave cloth or make pots. And no, I am not attracted to female bodies.

"I know not what it is, but I feel something coming that will take me away. I do not feel I belong here. In my dreams, I see Bright Star, you, and all the others with happy lives full of children and good things. I am nowhere in those dreams. The gods have something else planned for me," Cass said.

"You cannot know what, if anything, the gods wish for you. Do not talk of such things. Perhaps you just need more time to adjust. We will not push you, for now," Corn Stalk relented.

Cass was up early and felt the warm, damp air

the instant she pulled the blanket from her sweaty body. She wore her thin sleeping dress to go out to tend to her natural needs. As soon as she pulled the door hanging aside, the young woman was surprised. Not only had the temperature increased dramatically, but the humidity had skyrocketed. A fog so thick it was a challenge to count the fingers on her hand at the end of her outstretched arm, had descended on the land. Planting and hunting would have to wait.

She felt her way out to the latrine pit and thanked the Creator when she was finished and returned to the longhouse without falling in. She had to feel her way every step, going and coming back.

Cass noticed Bright Star awake and went to talk to her sister. "The fog is so thick, you need a guide to get to the piss hole," Cass quipped.

"I cannot smell it on you, so I guess you did not fall in," Bright Star chuckled.

"More by good luck," Cass replied. "Looks like planting will be delayed."

"Are you really going hunting?" Bright Star asked.

"That was my plan, but now, who knows when that fog will lift. The air is as still as inside a box."

"They really think you are two spirit?" Bright Star snickered.

"I could not care less what those miserable snakes think about me," Cass snarled.

"They are just frustrated because you will not even talk to them about courting. They are men, they have their manhood to exercise."

"I have not caught you exercising any of them, either. Eh?"

"No, and you won't, for now. I do not know why not though. Red Hand is gone, so I have nothing else to wait for. Running Wolf is handsome, although he is one who has said you are two spirit. Any man who insults my sister is not for me. He apologized quickly and said it was only a joke," Bright Star scoffed.

"You talked to him about me? When?" Cass was suddenly agitated.

"Relax. He came around when you were talking to Corn Stalk yesterday. He was plenty coy. I am not sure if he came to court you or me. I told him maybe by Solstice, one of us might be willing to talk," Bright Star said conspiratorially.

"I know you do not believe me, but Red Hand is your future. I cannot say when or how, just that the two of you have made an appearance in many of my dreams," Cass said cautiously.

"That old story. It is getting harder to believe every day. I am sorry if you do not like me saying so, but I do not like you giving me hope when there is none."

"Soon, something will happen soon. I can feel it," Cass replied.

"So, guide me out to the piss hole, since you have already found it in the fog," Bright Star demanded.

When Cass pulled back the door hanging, the visibility had improved to about two paces as the dawn approached. She and Bright Star fumbled their way along the longhouse wall until their noses told them they were close. Cass waited, standing against the sloping bark wall, while Bright Star did her personal business.

While Cass was waiting, Water Mint came along with Fingerling hanging onto her dress and Dewdrop in her arms. "What are you doing standing out here?" Water Mint asked Cass.

"Oh, Bright Star needed a guide in this fog, is all," Cass replied snidely.

"All right. As long as you are here, you help Fingerling take care of his business while I take care of myself and Dewdrop, please" Water Mint said, not taking 'no' for an answer.

"By the way, Tallow told me that if I saw you, he is going to work on making some stone trade goods this morning. He said you would be crazy to go hunting in this weather. He will be out by the plaza fire pit in a hand of time or so."

"Tell him I will be there. Come on Fingerling, let us find the hole and hope neither of us falls in," Cass said jovially.

Cass and Fingerling were making their way back to the east entrance of the large, oval-shaped longhouse when they met Corn Stalk on her way to do her morning business.

"Does not look like an ideal planting day, Head Matron," Cass greeted Corn Stalk.

"It has already lifted some, Cass. I think we will be in the fields in a hand of time. The path is well-worn to the fields, and we can surely find our way from mound to mound. Are you joining us? Not much of a day for hunting," Corn Stalk asked.

"As it turns out, I will join Tallow in the plaza. We are going to work on making stone trade goods. I need to keep my flint knapping skills honed if I am ever going to be a good wife," Cass joked.

Corn Stalk smiled and shook her head as she passed them. *She insists on doing man's work. I know she will make many more arrow points than scrapers and women's knives.*

CHAPTER 27
TALLOW

C ass and Tallow sat on logs near the east-facing entrance of the Corn Clan longhouse. They were engaged in making trade goods in the form of stone tools and weapons. The trade goods were in preparation for the Solstice Celebration, just over a moon away.

Cass wore a plain, brown fabric, sleeveless hunting shirt. It was mostly faded to a dark tan color, and though clean, it bore stains from many animal cleanings and processing. The shirt hung nearly to her knees. Under her shirt was a thin, gray-colored doeskin loincloth tied at the waist with a rawhide thong. Her feet were covered with ankle-high moccasins. She wore a coarse hemp-fiber sash, tied above her left hip, that held two small leather pouches, her sheathed obsidian knife, a hand-long bone stiletto slid crosswise into the hemp fibers along her flat belly, and her ever-present war club. One of her small leather pouches carried her clay pipe and smoking materials. The other held a chert woman's knife, a small bundle of shredded cedar bark tinder, and two black stones with yellow flakes that would cast off a spark when struck together for igniting a fire.

Her hair was now nearly a fingernail long over her entire head. It resembled the pin feathers on a fledgling crow. Cass had little use for bejeweled clothing, hair decorations, tattoos, or face paint. Even without those things, she was well known for her stunning beauty and athletic body, although she had lived in Monongahela Village for less than a moon.

To her side lay a woven grass basket that held smaller bags. One, made of tanned elk skin, contained her knapping tools. Another, made of deerskin, held several blank nodules of various colors and types of chert from quarries near and far, a few obsidian blanks, and some assorted crystal chunks also from faraway places. The last bag, made from a tanned otter skin with the hair turned in, held finished products. Each class of products was wrapped in its own rabbit skin. The arrow points were in one skin, lance points in another, and so on.

Tallow wore a light tan-colored buckskin vest with fringe along the bottom hem just above his waist. Deer Clan symbols were painted on the front and back. His fringed, brown-tanned breechclout hung below mid-thigh and was held up by rawhide thongs. A tied leather belt held two small leather pouches, similar to the ones Cass wore, a sheathed chert knife, and his war club.

His hair was divided into two braids that hung down his chest on each side. The braids were tied with plain brown leather thongs. Deer Clan tattoos adorned his temples and forehead, and a black geometric band ran from ear to ear and over the bridge of his nose.

At his side were bags like the ones Cass had.

Tallow was amazed and a little jealous of the skill Cass exhibited in her flint knapping. She could pick up a nodule of any stone that could be shaped by flaking, turn it in her hands, study it briefly, and go to work. She could envision the tool or weapon hidden in the stone. She seemed to instinctively know just how to pick out the subtle shoulders on the rock and where to strike it with which tool, and how hard. She seldom made a mistake, and her tools and weapons always traded well. Of course, Tallow had to claim her things were his work and trade them as his own. Women were forbidden from making anything beyond scrapers and women's knives.

By mid-morning, the dense fog had lifted above the palisade walls but still obscured the tops of the taller trees and the surrounding hills. The air was so still, smoke rose straight up and blended with the low-hanging clouds. The warm, humid air seemed to cling to everything. Sweat came easily and soaked clothing rapidly. The heavy air discouraged evaporation.

This was the first day of warm temperatures, which brought hordes of buzzing and biting insects. Cass and Tallow wore a heavy layer of bear fat mixed with juniper berry juice and mint covering all exposed skin areas. In addition, they kept their clay pipes lit in hopes of deterring the voracious bugs.

Wreaths of gray-tan smoke hung around them in layers. Their supplies of tobacco were depleted, and they were filling their clay pipes with a substitute made by collecting black and riverbank willow leaves during a previous growing season. The hard stems were nipped off and the leaves placed in a large pot of simmering, but not boiling, water sweetened with honey. Once the leaves were saturated, they were placed on a wooden drying rack over a smoky, cherrywood fire until the leaves were dried crispy. Next, the dried leaves were put on a metate and crushed with a grinding stone. Once crushed, the leaf flakes were poured into ceramic jars and fitted with wooden plugs. When full, the plugs were inserted and sealed with melted beeswax. The jars were then marked and stored until needed. When tobacco supplies were depleted the jars of tobacco substitutes were available. This substitute was not tobacco and did not have the spirit and thick blue smoke of tobacco, but the sweetened smoke was not unpleasant to inhale, and it helped keep the insects at bay.

"You have been putting all the young hunters to shame with your successful hunts," Tallow complimented Cass. He kept one eye on her, and one on his own work.

"You know deer are plentiful in this valley. There are decent numbers of elk around as well. Bears and mountain lions are not hard to find. Turkeys and ruffed grouse are numerous. The spirits treat us well here," Cass replied nonchalantly.

"I assume you still thank each animal as you take it?"

"Of course, and that may be why I am usually successful." She looked up from the ceremonial knife she was working on. *Is he insinuating something?*

"You know there are rumors floating around

about you?" Tallow asked when he saw her look him in the eye. *I need to distract her. I cannot let her think I was admiring her thighs and sweat-soaked breasts.*

"I have heard some things," Cass replied as if she did not care. Her eyes went back to her work.

"You also know Corn Stalk desperately wants to get you married so you will rejoin the Clan and become more normal. A marriage would silence the rumors. That is a fact."

With her concentrating on the rose-quartz knife blade she was shaping, his eyes went back to her inner thighs. He could see to the side of her loincloth where a few black hairs were visible along the edge at the top of her legs. His manhood responded to the sight, and the thought of coupling with her dominated his thoughts. *I am not even an adopted uncle, technically. A mating between us would not be considered incest.* Tallow justified his lust in his own mind.

Tallow had been close to Cass since the raid on Long Pine Village. He had watched her grow from a scrappy child to a beautiful young woman with more talents than he could count. He personally instructed her in many of her skills. But she took each one of the things he taught her to a higher level. *She truly is an amazing young woman.* Yes, he loved his wife and children. But a man in his position with two or more wives was not uncommon. *There is no reason I should not take Cass for a second wife.*

"Cass, there is a simple solution to your problem. Since we are all under the same roof and have been living that way for many sun cycles, we could just declare that you are my second wife."

"What!?" she retorted, her hands going still for the first time since they started working earlier in the morning.

"It only makes sense. Nothing would change. We just continue as we have been all along. No one needs to know it is not so. The rumors and snide remarks would go away, and we would all be happier. No one will ask anything of you of an intimate nature. And you would be free to find a real mate when you feel comfortable," Tallow said. To him, it all sounded logical. *And, you will be welcome in my bed anytime,* he did not say out loud.

Cass carefully put her tools and paraphernalia away, stood, and turned her back on Tallow. She did not want him to see the anger in her eyes. She stood, back straight and arms folded tightly under her firm breasts.

How could he suggest such a thing? It must be his manhood dominating his brain. Does he think I would agree to such a stupid idea? And how does he think Water Mint would take such an arrangement? Bright

Star would be livid if she heard what just came out of Tallow's mouth.

"Cass. Think about it. It would solve this issue with the rumors, and nothing needs to change," Tallow implored.

Cass looked up. High overhead a pale disk, visible in the dull gray sky for only a few heartbeats, told her the day was about half over.

CHAPTER 28
SPROUT'S MESSAGE

The patter of small feet running bare across the hard-packed plaza trail came near. Cass spun around, clutching the handle of her war club, to see Sprout, Corn Stalk's youngest grandson, running around the curved wall of the longhouse and toward Tallow. The boy wore only a small loincloth. At seven summers, he was fast for his age. His skin glistened with bear grease and sweat. His feet and lower legs were covered with mud.

Sprout stopped in front of Tallow and burst out between huffing gasps, "Warrior, canoes are coming downriver! A big warrior in the front carries a white arrow." Sprout's hands were braced on his knees as he tried to catch his breath.

Cass yelled out, "They are here!" She turned, stepped over, and dropped to one knee just behind Sprout. She clutched his narrow shoulders and spun him around to look him in the eye.

"You must hurry to the planting fields and tell Grandmother Corn Stalk, Water Mint, and Bright Star about the canoes. Run as fast as you can! You will do that?" Cass implored.

The boy just looked at her hand on his left shoulder. A tear formed in his eye. His little chest was heaving, sucking in all the air he could.

She looked and saw that she had unwittingly pinned the hot bowl of her clay pipe against his shoulder. She withdrew the pipe as quickly as she could and blew a breath of air across the red spot on the boy's upper arm.

"Sorry. If you run like the wind, it will cool this down and make you very brave. Go now, go tell the women! I will make sure you get extra sweetened corn cakes with the evening meal." Cass did not give the boy, or Tallow, a chance to question her. She pointed the boy toward the man-gate along the southeast palisade wall and shoved him in that direction.

Cass quickly gathered her things into her reed basket.

"Who is here?" Tallow asked.

"It is Red Hand. He is here for my sister's hand!" Cass exclaimed joyfully. Her anger at Tallow had disappeared like a puff of smoke on a windy day.

"How can you know that?" he queried.

Shouldering her bag, she turned toward the entrance of the Corn Clan longhouse.

"I know," she said.

"Wait, I'll go with you!"

Her anger came back, and Cass replied sharply, "You should get some men together and go hunt some deer or an elk for a couple of days of feasts." With that, she turned and disappeared though the door hanging.

Tallow began putting his knapping things away. Cass emerged from the longhouse in just a few heartbeats, turned, and strode purposefully toward the main palisade opening. He watched her graceful motions and tried to conjure a way he could coax her into his sleeping skins. He watched her rocking hips until she was through the opening. *She is every man's dream.*

Then, it dawned on him that he had better get his bow and quiver and find someone to hunt with him. The last thing he wanted was to disappoint Cass. Looking around, he saw several men working in pairs, straightening arrow shafts, gluing fletching feathers on arrows, and other such tasks. He noted that all work stopped, and all eyes followed her until Cass was out of sight. In a short time, he had a hunting party organized and started out to find some game.

CHAPTER 29
TRAVELER RETURNS

Cass cleared the palisade and looked down the path toward the canoe landing. The palisade stood about two long bow shots from the riverbank. This day, the river was full to the bank, and the canoes laid on the bank in full view.

Just as a canoe slid to a stop, Cass caught movement to her right. There, she saw Red Oak leading a party of warriors with strung bows and nocked arrows moving toward the landing. Red Oak was Corn Stalk's oldest grandson and already a leader in the warrior society of Monongahela Village.

Cass ran to him, then at his side as they approached the landing. "What is happening?" she called out to Red Oak.

"Black Bear warriors approach. We will make sure they come in peace," Red Oak replied proudly.

"They come in peace, cousin. Red Hand is here to ask for my sister's hand," Cass answered confidently.

"How can you know that? They are just arriving. We know there are four canoes," he answered.

"I know!" she replied. "You can put away your bows. But your men can help carry their belongings to the Corn Clan longhouse." Red Oak ordered his followers to put their weapons away without thinking why he listened to Cass.

As they approached the first canoe, Cass called out, "Red Hand, my heart sings to see you! Welcome to Monongahela Village!"

"Cass? Is that you? I did not expect to see you at the landing of such a big village, nor did I expect you to be chosen to welcome a party from Black Bear Village!" Red Hand replied, with puzzlement in his voice and written on his face.

She walked right up and hugged him. "Ha! There is much conjecture about how long I will be welcome in this village. And I am nobody here. When we returned, my aunt and her husband had moved our belongings to the Head Matron's longhouse, so we are here, for now. I got wind that you were arriving and came out on my own to make sure some overzealous young warriors did not use you for target practice."

Cass let her remarks sink in as she watched another canoe arrive. "You can tell me who you have brought, but just informally. Formal introductions will take place in the village. The warrior here is Red Oak. He is Head Matron Corn Stalk's grandson and son of War Chief Wolf Master. He is a fine warrior. Red Oak and his men will help bring your things into the village."

Red Hand shook his head. "As usual, Cass, you are full of surprises. In this first group, we have Night Owl, Head Matron of Black Bear Village—"

Night Owl interrupted Red Hand, "So, this is Cass? All Black Bear Village owes you a debt of gratitude, maiden. On behalf of all our people, we thank you."

Cass noted that the Head Matron had seen perhaps four-tens-and-five summers. She wore a plain traveling dress, with only a bear painted on the chest. Her graying hair was pulled up in a bun on the back of her head and pinned with bone skewers. She wore bear and geometric tattoos on her squarish face, and circles around her upper arms. She had several copper and bead bracelets on each arm.

"I was only following orders from Wolf,

Matron. But I am humbled by your gratitude," Cass replied, dipping her head.

"The rest of our party, then. First is Ten Point, the new War Chief of Black Bear Village. He is married to the sister of the former Great War Chief. She could not come because she will soon deliver her second child."

Cass looked at Ten Point with worry in her eyes.

Noting her discomfort, Ten Point offered, "Do not worry, maiden. Cool Dawn had no love for her half-brother. He harmed her as he did others."

Cass nodded in understanding but did not speak.

Night Owl continued, "Stepping out of the next canoe, the gray-haired man is Red Loon. He is of the Heron Clan and is my husband. The woman is Goldeneye, Head Matron of the Heron Clan, and mother of Red Hand. I think you have met Two Hearts of the Deer Clan. Our last canoe, just approaching, has Cold Duck, Heron Clan, and Many Feathers, Hawk Clan," Night Owl stated quickly. She was surprised to see Many Feathers had changed into his ceremonial clothing, as if this meeting at the canoe landing was of some extraordinary importance.

Cass noted the last canoe full of tanned skins

and several reed baskets. She turned to Red Hand, "You are here on a trade mission?"

"In a manner. I did not know what to expect for a bride price, so we came prepared," Red Hand replied.

"Ha! I think *you* could have my sister for one green, summer woodrat hide. But it is not my place to decide such things. And I thought you were already married?" Cass replied.

"My former wife died in childbirth, along with the child. It happened during the big blizzard," Red Hand answered solemnly.

"Red Hand?" Many Feathers called as he stepped too close to Cass.

Cass noted the tall warrior was a handsome one. He wore fine skins and sported many tattoos. Then, she saw the look in his eye. Predatory. His eyes were focused on her breasts, plainly through her sweaty, wet shirt.

"Whom must Many Feathers seek to ask permission to court this young maiden?" Many Feathers called out, never diverting his eyes from Cass's breasts.

"I can answer that question, Red Hand," Cass replied over her shoulder as she looked into Many Feathers' eyes.

He looked briefly at her face, then focused back on her breasts.

"Many Feathers, is it?" Cass started, then continued, "If my mother, and all the matrons in my lineage, came back from the Land of the Ancestors and stood behind me, they would say, 'Many Feathers, you are a handsome one. We can tell from your tattoos you are a great warrior. And your fine clothing says you would provide a good life for this maiden. Of course, you have our permission to court our daughter.' Even *if* all that was said, the answer would still be 'No!' You do not have permission to court this maiden," Cass said matter-of-factly.

Just then, motion caught her eye. Through the trees on the riverbank to the east, she glimpsed another canoe. *It is a bark canoe, a trader's canoe!* She noted the white hand painted on the front. Through the trees, she saw the rear paddler. *Traveler!*

Cass turned and left Many Feathers and the Black Bear Villagers with their mouths agape. Noting the first opening in the long row of overturned canoes, she ran to get there before the canoe gliding downriver in the fast-moving current. She would need to hurdle seven boats before arriving at the opening.

A LOOK AT BOOK FOUR
WESTWARD

In a journey that intertwines fate and survival, two warrior souls bound by destiny face an uncertain future.

After avenging the brutal murder of her parents by destroying the ruthless war chief Thunder Throat, Cass, a fierce and determined young woman, believes her fight is finally over. But a chance encounter with Yellow Hair, a Norseman washed ashore and raised in lands controlled by the Lenni Lenape People, sets her on a new path—one that will take her far beyond the safety of her village.

Joined by the enigmatic trader, Traveler, the trio embarks on a dangerous expedition to Cahokia, a burgeoning city rich with power and politics. Tasked with delivering Yellow Hair to the Great Sun, Traveler's mission is fraught with peril, and the journey ahead is one of both discovery and survival.

For Cass and Yellow Hair, their dreams of a peaceful life together are threatened by forces beyond their control. From violent storms to enemies new and old, the odds seem insurmountable. Yet, together, they must navigate treacherous terrain and the political intrigues of Cahokia if they are to forge a future against all odds.

Embark on a timeless odyssey as two fierce warriors battle against the forces of nature, enemies, and fate itself.

AVAILABLE DECEMBER 2024

ACKNOWLEDGMENTS

Thanking all the people who inspired, encouraged, and supported a person who writes a book is a daunting task. It is akin to writing a comprehensive history of the world. And no matter how hard one tries; important influencers are left out in these efforts. People like that third grade teacher who taught you how to punctuate a sentence, the milk man who delivered the milk no matter what the weather was doing, the wrestling coach who made you get back on the mat, no matter how badly the last opponent beat you, the brothers and sisters who taught you the importance of teamwork and loyalty, the father who demonstrated that you always get up and go to work, regardless of your problems or rewards, and the mother who showed you that the most important thing in life is love.

I wish to thank my family for making me who I am, my instructors for teaching me how to think, my friends for their support and encouragement, and every author I have ever read for inspiring me to put my own thoughts on paper.

ABOUT THE AUTHOR

Ron Briggs is a veteran, having served four years in the USAF. His education includes a Bachelor of Science in Range and Wildlife Ecology at Oklahoma State University and a Master of Science in Range and Wildlife Management at Texas A&I University.

He is retired from the USDA-Natural Resources Conservation Service, and his career encompassed twenty-five years as District Conservationist in Linn County, Kansas. Prior to college, he worked seven years in the building trades.

Having developed a deep interest in history, especially in the pre-colonial period of North America, Ron's interests prompted him to begin researching a pre-history story about the Tallgrass Prairie Region of the Great Plains. That research evolved into his current multi-volume work, the Yellow Hair series, which includes scenes from northern Europe to the mountains of western North America.

Ron and his wife, Debbie, currently live in Mound City, Kansas, and have two grown children and seven grandchildren. His interests include spending time with family, writing, hunting, fishing, traveling, and woodworking.

BIBLIOGRAPHY

Bierhorst, John. *Mythology of the Lanape: Guide and Texts.* University of Arizona Press, 1995.

Charles River Editors. *Native American Tribes: The History and Culture of the Innuit (Eskimos).* 2013.

Damas, David and William C. Sturtevant, eds. *Handbook of North American Indians.* Vol. 5-Arctic, Smithsonian Press, 1985.

Grumet, Robert S. *The Lenapes (Indians of North America).* Chelsea House, 1989.

Harrington, Mark R. *Religion and Ceremonies of the Lenape.* Forgotten Books, 2012.

--. *The Indians of New Jersey, Dickon Among the Lanapes.* Rutgers University Press, 1963.

Heckewelder, John Gotlieb Ernestus, notes by William C. Reichel. "History, Manners, and Customs of The Indian Nations Who Inhabited Pennsylvania and the Neighbouring States." Historical Society of Pennsylvania, 1881.

--. "The Family Hunting Territory and Lenape Political Organization." American Anthropology 24, 1922.

Means, Bernard K. *Circular Villages of the Monongahela Tradition.* University of Alabama Press, 2007.

Trigger, Bruce G. *Handbook of North American Indians, Volume 15-Northeast.* Smithsonian Press, 1984.

Weslager, C. A. *The Delaware Indians: A History.* Rutgers University Press, 1972.

www.ingramcontent.com/pod-product-compliance
Lightning Source LLC
Chambersburg PA
CBHW011516240626
47154CB00010B/3051